The Wartime Winter

Joseph Curry

MOGZILLA

The Wartime Winger

ISBN: 9781906132156

Text copyright: Joseph Curry.
Cover by Zillamog
Cover ©Mogzilla 2016
Printed in the UK.
First published by Mogzilla in 2016

http://www.mogzilla.co.uk/

Author's dedication:

For Esther, Owen and Aidan

Chapter 1

Liam had lived next door to the old man for three years before they ever spoke a word to each other. Watching through a crack in his parent's fence, he'd often seen him planting flowers in his back garden and moving about in the shed in the far corner. But, if he was absolutely honest about it, the old man scared him a little with his bushy, silvery eyebrows and thick hair that looked like it had never been combed. Occasionally their eyes had met but Liam had looked away quickly before there had been an opportunity to strike up a conversation. The old man didn't really look like the chatty type anyway.

It probably would have remained that way too if it hadn't been for Morgan Harris. Liam couldn't stand that kid. He had a mouth the size of the channel tunnel, always winding people up and stirring up trouble. It had been exactly the same this morning and Liam had been furious when he'd arrived home early from the match. He'd always had trouble controlling his temper and his anger just seemed to overpower him at times. He'd always regret it afterwards but by the time the day was over he was glad that he'd kicked Morgan Harris. It had led to him being in just the right place at just the right time...

Liam was ten and full of resentment. He was the youngest of four brothers living in the North-East of England and life was never quite what he wanted it to be. His father had left the family home when Liam was just two years old and barely had any contact with him, while his mother struggled to give the required attention to four lively boys with just seven years separating them in age.

Most days were a diet of disappointments. School wasn't great and he had no friends. Many of the teachers were kind to him but he always ended up letting them down somehow and he would hate himself for being so weak-willed. He'd often start a piece of writing really well and begin to feel like learning wasn't so difficult. But things always went wrong. He'd make a spelling mistake that another pupil would point out or he'd lose concentration and make a mess of his handwriting. Before he could control it, his anger would take over and he would rip up his book or scribble through his work. For the rest of the week, he would play the fool and put in minimum effort. The fear of failure was crippling and the hurt and anger would grow stronger.

In fact, the only lesson that Liam excelled in was PE. He didn't mind gymnastic lessons and had always been a strong runner since his days in Mrs Jackson's reception class. However, it was in ball sports that he demonstrated a natural talent. He was an excellent cricketer and a powerful rugby player but as a footballer he had always stood out from his peers. Being part of the school team filled him with pride and for once in his life he actually felt like he belonged. It was probably the only reason that he could cope with school at all and on a match day he would barely be able to contain his excitement.

Today had been no exception. The game against Riverside Primary had kicked off at two o'clock and Liam had been having a great match, crunching into tackles as if his life depended on it and firing in powerful shots from all angles. At half time the score had been one all and Mr James, the school football coach, had been pleased. He'd complimented Liam on his performance and reminded him not to respond to the sly taunts of Morgan Harris, the opposition captain.

Morgan Harris was well known as the league's wind up merchant. He was small in stature, with short spiky hair and mischievous eyes. Although he was a talented player himself, he couldn't resist having a dig at any opponents who crossed his path. There were often sly elbows when the referee's back was turned and a constant stream of sarcastic comments seemed to flow from his mouth.

Perhaps sensing that Liam had a temper, he had targeted him in the first half, treading on his toes deliberately at corners and sarcastically applauding shots that trickled wide of goal. Liam had resisted the temptation to retaliate until mid-way through the second half, with the scores still level. Harris had tripped him to the floor, before lifting him to his feet in a show of false concern. In the process, and out of view of the referee, Harris had dug his nails into the skin of Liam's armpits and scratched them painfully.

Before he could check himself, Liam lashed out, kicking Morgan Harris in his right calf. The referee didn't really have a choice and pulled out the inevitable red card. Liam's match had ended prematurely and the shame, anger and resentment began to surge through his veins. He'd let everyone down again. Blinded by burning tears and still in full kit he stormed home.

Small drops of rain had started to fall by the time Liam reached home. No-one was there. His mother was at the White Lion where she worked as a barmaid and goodness knows what his three brothers were up to. They rarely arrived home before seven. Undeterred by the rain, Liam headed for the back garden. Finding his battered old football, he began lashing it against the back wall, pretending it was Morgan Harris' shins. This was the second time he'd been sent off this season and Mr James had warned him that he was on his last chance. He'd blown it now. There was nothing to look forward to anymore.

Harder and harder he struck the football at the wall, almost working himself into a frenzied rage. The skies had grown an angry dark colour and he was dripping wet now. Finally, he struck the ball so hard that it rebounded off the wall and over the fence, landing in the garden next door. Liam stood still for a moment. The old man usually threw the ball back after a few weeks but he didn't really want to wait that long. Still a little afraid of his neighbour, he hesitated. It was pouring with rain. Surely the old man couldn't see much through his windows and he'd only be there for a matter of seconds. His heart racing, he climbed up the fence and jumped down into next door's garden.

Chapter 2

Glancing around anxiously, Liam grabbed the old football. He was just about to throw it back over the fence when he heard a voice from behind him.

"What do you think you're doing?"

Liam turned sharply. The old man stood at the doorway, scrutinising him through piercing blue eyes. His face was wrinkled and unshaven. He seemed to have no control over his mop of unruly hair while a thick scar snaked its way down the left side of his forehead.

"You must be crazy staying outside in this weather," the old man said, his voice a little gentler now, "and what are you banging that football so hard for? You're going to bring that wall down if you carry on."

Liam said nothing and didn't move.

The old man smiled warmly and suddenly he didn't seem so threatening.

"I must say that you do strike the ball well," he continued, "right off the laces and straight as an arrow. Just like I used to."

Liam stood there open mouthed and shivering. He must have looked a sorry sight.

"It's Liam isn't it?" the old man said softly. "I've heard your mother calling you in from the garden on quite a few occasions over the last few years. Never listen either do you? Always needing to take one more shot."

Liam blinked the rain from his eyes and met the old man's gaze. He couldn't stop staring at the scar on his forehead.

"Look Liam," the old man said. "I've just made a hot chocolate and you look like you could do with one too. Why don't you get out of the rain for a minute and join me? I'm Jimmy by the way. Jimmy Evans."

Liam followed the old man into his house and into a small lounge. A small Jack Russell dog slept by a blazing fire. While the old man busied himself in the kitchen next door, Liam enjoyed the warmth of the fire and studied the room. Like their owner, the sofa and matching chairs had probably seen better days, and the walls could have done with a lick of paint. A small television sat on an ancient wooden cabinet and a ragged, old mat covered part of a carpet. It looked like the sort of room you would expect an old man living on a small pension to have. As he heard footsteps coming along the hallway, Liam caught a glimpse of two old photographs, positioned on the windowsill. One was of a couple, in their early thirties, with three young children, whereas the other was of two smiling young men in rather strange looking football gear.

"I was much better looking in those days you know." The old man stood in the doorway, holding a tray containing two mugs of hot chocolate and a few jammy dodger biscuits. Liam stood frozen, a little embarrassed that he'd been caught snooping.

"Take a seat," the old man said, motioning for him to sit down in the chair facing the fire, "and make sure you don't steal all the jammy dodgers or there'll be trouble." Liam nodded nervously, failing to notice that the old man had been joking.

"The first picture is of my wife and children," the old man said with a smile. My three are all grown up these days. They've got busy lives and their own families to worry about. My youngest grandchild is the same age as you. The lady on the left is my lovely wife Angie and in case you're wondering, the handsome fellow in the middle is me."

The old man saw Liam thinking for a minute and read his thoughts.

"Oh, I lost Angie some time ago. I'm on my own now. I've just got Sam for company," he said quietly, pointing at the sleeping dog.

Finding his voice at last, Liam couldn't help asking about the second photograph.

"You said that you used to play football too."

"A very long time ago," the old man replied, smiling a little. "My pace lets me down these days. I have to make do with watching *Match of the Day* on the box or taking in a game at the local playing fields while I'm walking Sam."

Liam took a bite of a jammy dodger and a slurp of hot chocolate.

"I've even seen you playing a few times," the old man continued. "You're a good little player. Great left foot, powerful runner and a lovely first touch – you just get a bit too fiery sometimes – let people get under your skin."

Liam looked down at his feet for a moment. He wondered how many times the old man had seen him lashing out at opponents, arguing with the referee or storming off. He felt a sharp prickle of shame.

The old man caught Liam's eye.

"Don't be ashamed of who you are Liam," he said. "It's good to have that fire in your belly and determination to succeed. You've just got to keep control of your temper. Remember that football's a team game and you can't help your team if you're not on the pitch."

Liam stared at the photograph of the two football players.

"Were you any good when you played?" he asked a little nervously. "You know – did you ever win anything?"

His blues eyes shimmering for a second, the old man laughed. "I did alright for myself," he replied. "Won a few things - could have won more with a little more luck."

Curious but a little reluctant to pry, Liam's eyes were drawn to the two footballers in the photograph.

"Who's that in the picture with you," he asked, slightly fearful of the answer.

"That's my friend Stan," the old man replied. "The best footballer I ever played with and the bravest person I ever knew."

He picked up the photo frame from the windowsill and slumped back in his chair.

"I'll tell you about him if you like."

Liam nodded.

"It's a bit of a story. Are you sure you've got the time?"

Liam nodded again and the old man sat up in his seat, his eyes still on the photograph. He spoke in a slow, measured tone, choosing his words carefully.

Chapter 3

Well Liam, being punched in the face doesn't normally lead to anything good I guess, but when I look back now it was the best thing that could have happened to me. It led to me meeting the best friend I ever had. It was 1930, with winter drawing to an end, when I was struck by a burly eleven year old named Billy Graham. I had been at school for three weeks.

With blood pouring from my lower lip, I looked up at my attacker in terror. Billy Graham was a schoolyard bully who had obviously spotted easy pickings in me. I suppose I was a soft target, being a slight, nervous looking boy with unwashed hair. Within seconds, he was towering above me, his left hand balled into a tight fist.

"Let's see it then you skinny piece of dirt," he glowered.

"See what," I managed to answer, my heart pumping through my chest.

"Your money," Graham growled. "You're going to have to get used to the rules at this school sooner or later. Rule number one is that when you see me, you got to give me money. Even an idiot like you can remember that."

"I have no money," I whispered. My breath stuck in my throat and I had to strain over every word.

I remember the blow that followed bringing tears to my eyes and leaving my legs trembling.

"I haven't got any money," I repeated as a crowd of smirking children watched from a distance.

Graham rested a hand on my shoulders, squeezing more and more tightly.

"That's alright," he replied. "I'll take your shoes. If you've got no money, I'll take them instead. My kid brother could do with a new pair."

I stared at the older boy, not quite comprehending what I was being asked.

"You can't have my shoes – my mother's just bought them for me," I whimpered.

Graham glared back at me.

"Either I take them shoes or you take home a broken nose."

"I can't give you my shoes," I whimpered, the tears streaming down my reddened cheeks. "I just can't."

Without further hesitation, Graham unloaded three savage blows to my head, knocking me to the floor. He followed up with a kick in the ribs, forcing the air out of my lungs.

"You're gonna end up dead for those stupid shoes," Graham muttered, preparing to unleash further damage. Speckles of blood had emerged on my school shirt. The crowd of children had grown larger but not one person had stepped in to halt the one-sided contest. Finally, after what seemed an eternity, a boy about my age pushed his way forwards. His name was Stan Whiteside.

Although, like me he was ten years old, Stan was a lot stronger, with broad shoulders and a tall wiry frame. Despite these attributes, he was still dwarfed by Billy Graham.

"He's had enough Billy," said Stan, positioning himself in between the two of us. "He's got the message."

"I'll decide when he's had enough," replied Graham. "Now run along home before someone else gets hurt."

"I'm not moving Billy. You can beat me senseless too if you like but I'm not sure Jack would like his younger brother coming home with a messed up face."

Graham stopped in his tracks momentarily. Everyone knew Stan's older brother Jack. He was fourteen years old and was well known as an up-and-coming boxer. It wouldn't be wise to take a swing at his younger sibling.

"You two aren't worth the skin off my knuckles anyway," said casually. "You can keep the shoes kid - for now anyway."

With that, he shuffled away, leaving Stan to pick me up from the floor and wipe the blood from my split lip...

Stan helped me to the first aid room where a stern looking woman with piercing coal black eyes glared down at me. Applying a cold compress to my head with all the tenderness of a bulldozer, she soon sent Stan and I on our way to class, without bothering to ask how the injuries had occurred.

It had been three weeks since I had arrived at Manorside Primary. Typically withdrawn, I had not really spoken to any of my classmates yet. I sat only two desks away from Stan but neither of us had spoken to each other before today.

"You didn't need to help me back there," I said softly, as we approached the classroom.

"I know that," Stan replied. "If I'd left you there for another five minutes, you'd have knocked him spark out. I was probably doing Billy Graham a favour. Our families go way back you know and his Mum would have been devastated if you'd ruined his pretty boy looks."

I looked at Stan, not knowing quite how to answer. Then we fell about in hysterics. I realised later that this was the first time I'd laughed in months.

Chapter 4

In the following two weeks Stan and I became firm friends. I never did like to talk about my family much back then but from what little I did say, Stan would remember me telling him that my father had abandoned the family home when I was very young and how we had moved to the area recently so my mother could take a new job. She worked night shifts at the time and I was often left to fend for myself, walking to school and making my own dinner. I was often ravenously hungry and people often told me that I could have done with a good wash. Stan would often say that a gust of wind could sweep me off my feet and he was probably right!

As spring began, Stan and I would walk home from school together most afternoons. Neither of us were the talkative sort and sometimes the mile long walk home could pass without more than the odd word. Looking back now, I realised that Stan recognised I was hiding something. He could sense it somehow but wouldn't say anything. It was two months after we met that he found out...

We had stayed late after school. I had to stay back after school as punishment for arriving late the previous day but Stan had waited for me anyway. It was half past six by the time we got to my street and the kitchen light was on. When I entered, my mother was sat at the table.

"I'm sorry I'm late Mum. I didn't think you'd be home," I said, slipping into my chair.

"That's alright love," she replied, staring through me vacantly. She slid my plate over to me.

"Thanks Mum. This looks good." She glanced at me, half smiling.

"I'm sorry love. I'm just a bit tired. I know I'm not much company."

I remember studying my mother's face. She was ghostly pale and her lips were so blue that it looked like the colour had been drained right out of them. I touched her arm tenderly.

"I'm doing OK at school Mum. I've made friends and I'm sure I've got better with my writing," I told her. She took a drink from her wine glass and leant back in her chair.

"My teachers think I've settled in well. I've just got to get to lessons on time and I won't have to go to any more detentions," I said. I regretted my words almost as they passed out of my lips.

"Detention," she thundered angrily. She checked herself quickly, knowing the neighbours would hear. "Detention," she hissed. "You're always letting me down Jimmy. Your father left me because of you. He loved me he did and you ruined it when you came along!"

"It was just a mix up Mum. I must have lost track of time."

"Are you arguing with me?" she threatened, anger overwhelming her. "Your own mother."

Before I could move out of the way, she had lurched

forward and slapped my face, sending me sprawling onto the floor. As I rose slowly to my feet, she retreated, almost immediately to the corner of the room, curled up in a ball, tears streaming down her face.

"I'm so sorry son," she whimpered. "I'm so sorry. I'm evil and I'm going to go to hell one day." I knew she was sorry. I knew she hated herself more every time she lost control. I knew that it would happen again. I put my arms around her and held her tight. I loved her so much. I still do – God rest her soul.

You see, it might not seem like it but my mother thought the world of me. She had two different cleaning jobs and would often have to leave me to fend for myself when I got home from school. I just don't think she could cope with being a single parent. She'd be the first to admit that. When my father left, her whole world just seemed to crumble and she became deeply depressed. There was just so much hurt and anger inside her for a few years and I guess I just bore the brunt of her frustration. Ninety-nine per cent of the time she was a caring, loving woman who was full of warmth and tenderness but there were just those few occasions when she became a different person. I don't like to think of my mother like that. That's not how I choose to remember her.

Anyway, as I looked to the window, I saw Stan in the street outside. He'd seen everything but in the following weeks he never uttered a word to me. I suppose he sensed that I couldn't bring myself to talk about it. Well, as the months passed and I got to know him, Stan became as loyal a friend that I could have wished for. Those of us who knew him well appreciated his unflappable personality. Nothing seemed to bother him and he had an inner confidence that could not be pierced. Behind his pleasant, boyish face lay a steel interior. Although he was an amiable boy and highly articulate, he preferred to be in a small group and actually preferred listening to others, rather than talking about himself. If he had a boiling point, it had yet to be discovered and although he was generally a quiet character he had a cheeky sense of humour.

Stan's quiet confidence had a calming influence on me. The quiet child lacking self-esteem gradually faded away. I'd always struggled to stand up for myself in the past, almost inviting bullies to walk all over me. Although my inner fears flickered inside my chest occasionally, I began to come out of my shell and become more assertive. Despite my small stature, I vowed I would never become anyone's victim ever again.

I soon learnt that Stan had one consuming passion. He was obsessed with football. Whenever he had a spare moment, Stan would be kicking a ball around, firing at indiscriminate objects such as plant pots or a neighbour's fence. He was very much like you actually Liam. People in his street would often complain but it was difficult to stay angry with Stan for too long.

That summer, the first ever FIFA World Cup was taking place and Stan studied the results in the newspapers. Although England had not yet decided to participate in this new event, Stan would tell me that he would lift the trophy one day.

"Imagine it Jim – champions of the world. That'd be alright wouldn't it," he'd say, pretending to hold a trophy above his head. I told him not to be so stupid. The World Cup would probably be held on the other side of the world. He'd have to fly on a plane and the thought of this terrified him.

Perhaps it was my friend's patient coaching or maybe it was a hidden natural talent, but I soon found myself becoming a handy player too. I developed a deadly left footed strike, could control the ball instantly and had the ability to glide gracefully past opponents at breakneck speed. It wasn't long before I joined Stan in representing the school team.

Chapter 5

In the early 1930s Stan and I spent every living moment kicking a ball around the local playing fields, pausing only to eat, sleep and go to school. We paid little attention to events unfolding in the world. In school, we learnt of scientists splitting the atom, read about the construction of the new Empire State building in America and chuckled at reports of a new food named the cheeseburger. News of a new German chancellor named Adolf Hitler barely registered in our sport obsessed minds.

Both of us each pushed the other to succeed. As we turned fourteen, Stan had developed into a powerful, cultured central midfielder with an eye for goal, while I was a lightning quick inside forward who scored bagfuls of goals. We had outgrown the school team and had graduated to representing the North East of England district eleven. Both of us were drawing the attention of first division giants Sunderland. Scouts were rumoured to be keen on attending the regional semi finals of the annual under 14's cup that was due to be played in three weeks time. Stan and I trained like we had never done before. It hadn't taken long until I shared my best friend's dream of playing for England. I didn't normally concentrate that well during lessons but I still remember something Mrs Griffiths, my English teacher had said when trying to motivate the class to take more interest in reading and writing.

"The more you dream children," she would say, "the further you will get and if you want to succeed, you have to do things that other people aren't willing to do." I did think she was talking rubbish at the time but I have to say this stuck with me for a long time.

Anyhow, on the way home from school the two of us would regularly discuss what tactics we would employ if we were to participate in the World Cup final and who would have the honour of captaining the side. We often had a penalty shoot out to decide this, each one deliberately putting the other off when we stepped up to the twelve yard spot. All it needed now was for the English FA to enter the competition.

So, as the weeks before the semi-final became days, we skipped school to work on our strength, speed and skill.

You have to do things that other people aren't willing to do!

We took turns to run the dreaded hillside zigzag path. This involved a lung-shredding burst up an impossible steep set of eighty-four steps (we had counted them carefully). If you were lucky enough to reach the top of the steps alive, there was a great view. However, it was difficult to enjoy it when you were bent over double on the point of throwing up. Still – it would be worth it when we got our first England caps!

To expand our lung capacity, as Stan had read this was important for athletes, we went to the local swimming baths. On the word go, each of us would dive to the bottom of the pool, grip hold of the side and just float there for as long as possible. Holding our breath, we would stay underwater for a little longer each time. Eventually, we could both manage approximately three minutes, although we were often interrupted by people diving in to save us.

The more you dream the further you will get.

Honing our shooting skills required meticulous preparation. Stan and I hung three dustbin lids from the garage roof of his back yard. Using a bright yellow paint, we inscribed a large one, two and three in the centre of them. For hours on end we would then strike Stan's old leather ball at them. We took it in turns to bellow out numbers while the other would have to fire a shot at the relevant target. We repeated this drill for volleys, free kicks and penalties. Stan even attempted an ambitious overhead kick that he'd once seen a skilful player try but that ended in glorious failure as it deflected off dustbin lid number three and straight through his neighbour's bathroom window!

So the semi-final drew ever closer and Stan and I dreamt bigger and bigger. In the days leading up to the match, I could barely focus on anything else. I felt great excitement but also a growing fear of what failure would mean. I didn't want to let anyone down and would lie awake for hours at night, worrying about playing badly. Of course, I know now that if you're afraid to fail, then you can never succeed. It's important to remember that Liam.

Chapter 6

It was a stormy March morning on the day of the big match but I knew I wasn't myself. An overpowering anxiety seemed to control my body and a tight knot had formed in the pit of my stomach. I had a sickening feeling that I was going to let the team down. My mood was as dark as the black sky outside. The rain was coming down from the heavens in thick sheets but the referee had inspected the pitch and deemed it fit to play on. It was five minutes until kick off and the pressure was suffocating.

"You'll be fine Jim," Stan whispered to me as the coach gave us his final instructions. I think he recognised how nervous I was and I wished I had his self belief. He seemed certain we would win.

"Just play your natural game and you'll tear them to shreds with you pace," he said, reassuring me. "I hope you don't get this nervous when we play in the World Cup final one day. Seriously – don't let anyone see that you're feeling tense. They'll think your weak and gain confidence themselves."

With that, we walked out onto the pitch, the rain lashing at our bare legs.

There are certain moments in life that seem frozen in time, forever etched in your memory. This was one of them. From the first whistle, the opposition were quicker to the ball than us, biting into tackles with venom and winning the ball. I wasn't really having a bad game; it was just that it seemed to pass me by. I was always on the periphery of the action and every time I received the ball, I was closed down quickly by eager and energetic midfield players.

Some of my team mates fared even worse. The match seemed to be a personal ordeal for one of our centre halves. Only fifteen minutes of the match had passed by when he failed to mark their striker from a corner. By the time our defence realised that there was a spare man at the back post, the goalkeeper was picking the ball out of the net.

I think some of their players picked up on how anxious our back four was. They sensed vulnerability and were absolutely merciless in exploiting any hesitation. We were in disarray and things were going from bad to worse. In the next attack, their nifty winger slalomed down the left flank and pulled the ball back. The cross should have been intercepted but inexplicably our centre half slipped at the vital moment. I could only watch as one of their midfielders struck a thunderbolt of a shot into the top corner of our net. At two nil down we had our backs against the wall, staring at defeat. As I trudged miserably back to the half-way line, I caught a glimpse of a man in an overcoat making notes. He had to be the scout from Sunderland. They all have a particular look about them. Anyway, there was no chance of him asking me for a trial. My spirits sank and I could feel my hopes sliding away.

Only Stan did himself justice. Calmly maintaining possession, putting his body on the line when making last ditch blocks and always encouraging team mates, he played with a maturity beyond his years. Despite his efforts, we trudged in at half time 3-0 down and in a sorry mess. There didn't seem to be any way back.

Disconsolate and in disbelief, we gathered in the changing rooms. Even our coach seemed to have given up. He went through the motions during the team talk. You know the sort of thing. We can get back into this with a bit of luck, and they'll soon tire in the second half. That sort of rubbish. We knew he didn't believe it. Not really. As we trudged out miserably for the second half, Stan gripped my arm. I'd never seen him angry before. He looked hurt and almost tearful.

"You've given up haven't you Jimmy," he said, struggling to control his emotions. "You've accepted they're better than us and you're going to wave the white flag. Let them walk all over you."

"Stan, I..." I stammered.

"What about England Jimmy? Our dreams. Dreams don't just happen do they. It takes sweat and determination – leaving everything you've got on the field. Never give in and never up." He stormed off, his face thunderous.

I still don't know what happened in the second half. Perhaps our opponents became complacent or maybe we found an urgency inspired by our own desperation but something was different. With Stan's words still ringing in my ears, I was fired up too. I began playing with a controlled fury, beating my marker to every ball, carrying out raids down the right flank and even winning the odd header.

After nine breathless minutes of the second half, we struck back. Stan swept in a towering high ball from a free kick and our centre forward glanced a header into the bottom right corner. I felt a surge of energy sweep through me. We could win this. They were anxious now and we had nothing left to lose. While we streamed forwards in numbers, the rain continued its savage onslaught. I'm still not sure how that game was ever finished in that weather!

About mid-way through the second half, we were camped outside the opposition penalty area. My confidence soaring, I received the ball about thirty yards from goal. Switching the ball from my right foot onto my left and turning sharply, I left the first defender for dead. A quick shimmy took care of the second and before I knew it I was staring into the whites of their goalkeeper's eyes. Time seemed to slow down as I stabbed my foot beneath the ball, lofting it over his head. I could hear virtually nothing. The silence was overwhelming. For a few agonising few moments, I was sure it was floating over the crossbar. It hung in the air, for what seemed an eternity, before drifting into the upper section of the net. Seventy years later and it's still my favourite goal. There was a certain beauty to it. Twenty minutes to go and we were back into it. Stan was the first to reach me, his smile telling its own story. I felt like I could faint but not from exertion. It was from the realisation of what I was capable of.

The match roared on to its conclusion and the rain finally relented. Bursts of sunlight squeezed through gaps in the clouds. Fifteen minutes to go, became ten minutes and before I knew it the ref was looking at his watch and ready to blow for full time. Stan won the ball with a crunching tackle on the half-way line and I was on the move almost immediately, timing my diagonal run to perfection to beat the offside trap. He struck the ball into the space between the opposition's centre halves and I was away. There was clear daylight between me and their last man. My heart thudded. My lungs were burning and my blood was roaring. Without breaking stride, I hit the ball with all my force.

To this day I still think that was the purest strike I ever hit. I could barely believe that the goalkeeper saved it. I still can't all these years later. The ball glided, almost gracefully, through the air and seemed destined for the top corner. It was one of those beautiful strikes that you know are going to burst the net from the moment the ball leaves your foot. Except this time it didn't. The goalkeeper made the save of his life, stretching every inch of his tall, rangy body to tip the ball onto the bar. I think it's still shaking now! Anyway, the whistle went almost instantly and I sank to the turf in dejection.

I don't know how long I lay collapsed on the turf but it felt like forever. Finally, I felt a hand grip my shoulder.

"Jimmy, don't take it to heart son," an unfamiliar voice said. "You couldn't have given any more and that's the sort of spirit I look for in a footballer. That and the other three S's – Stamina, speed and skill."

As I rose to my feet, I saw a stocky man with, kind eyes and a thick moustache.

"My name's George Smith," the man continued. "I represent Sunderland football club. "I'd like you and your friend Stan to attend a schoolboys' trial match at Roker Park next week." I think you've got half a chance of making something of yourself as a player."

"Be there for ten o'clock. And don't forget your boots!"

Chapter 7

To cut a long story short, the trial match went well. I notched up a couple of goals and Stan was his usual reliable self in central midfield, spraying passes from one side of the pitch to the other and controlling the tempo of the game from the first whistle. Sunderland signed us both on schoolboy forms that very afternoon.

Of course in those days, the transition between superstar schoolboy players to a full professional was not quite as smooth as it is nowadays. Both Stan and I left full time education before our fifteenth birthdays but we were too young to play senior football and would be forbidden to sign full professional terms until we were seventeen. There were no football apprenticeship schemes in those days although the odd player might be given a job on the ground staff, so Stan and I took jobs at the local timber yard to mark time. The days were long and the work was physically demanding but it kept us grounded I suppose. We lived for our football and never ever took it for granted.

I stuck it out in the North-East's junior football competitions for two achingly long years, followed by an eighteen month long baptism of fire in reserve league football. It was competitive to say the least, with bone crunching tackles the norm and regular threats of broken legs for skilful, pacy wide players like myself. I believe they call it character building. There was certainly no rolling about on the floor after the slightest touch that you see these days. No one would stand for that nonsense!

During these three years my whole life revolved around sport. I couldn't get enough of it. I listened as Italy won the second ever World Cup and I even watched Sunderland lift the league title. But the event that really stuck in my mind was the 1936 Olympics in Berlin.

Every day Stan and I would scour the papers for the latest news reports. The Germans and their leader Adolf Hitler had already shrouded the games in controversy by banning any Jewish athlete from the German team. America almost boycotted the games in protest and by the time they began in 1936, the whole world seemed to be holding its breath. Apparently, the usual 'Jews Not Welcome' signs normally seen throughout Germany were removed from hotels, restaurants and public places for the duration of the Olympics. Hitler obviously wanted to make a good impression.

I listened to the opening ceremony on the wireless as 100,000 filled the magnificent stadium. The Olympic torch arrived from Olympia, having been carried by an astonishing 3,000 runners over a twelve day period. The whole drama of it was intoxicating.

When the sporting competitions began, a young African American athlete named Jesse Owens became a superstar, winning four gold medals and setting world records in the process. For the next two weeks, he was my hero, defying Hitler's theories of a white master race. Stan and I even had a brief two week period of abandoning our World Cup dreams and becoming Olympians instead.

Anyway, I still remember that at the closing ceremony, the president of the International Olympic Committee requested the athletes of every country to gather once again in four years time in Tokyo. However, there would be no more Olympic Games for twelve years. The 1940 Games scheduled for Tokyo never took place. Instead of competing with each other on athletic fields, the youth of many countries wound up killing each other on the battlefield.

Chapter 8

Liam struggled to take in the old man's words for a minute. Did he really just say that athletes had ended up killing each other? How could that be? That couldn't have happened. He had so many questions but his mouth wouldn't obey his brain. He hadn't even finished his hot chocolate and it had now grown cold.

He sat there in silence before a familiar voice broke him out of his trance. "Liam! Liam! Are you out the back? I'm home. I've got us some chips for dinner."

Liam glanced at his watch. Time must have flown past and it was now seven o'clock.

The old man smiled. "You'd better get going," he said warmly, ushering Liam to the front door. "It's been great getting to know you Liam. Call by whenever you like. It's nice for me to talk to people you know. Sam's great company but he's not really the chatty sort."

Liam shut the front door behind him before hearing a knock at the window.

"Oh – and a good midfield player can run all day you know," the old man said. "Go easy on those chips!"

During the following morning's maths lesson, Liam's mind was racing as Mr Robson, his maths teacher, went through the finer points of column addition.

"Firstly make sure your digits are set out in the correct

place value columns."

The more you dream the further you will get.

Had Jimmy and Stan made it to the first team?

"Now begin to add up the units column and don't forget to carry the digits into the tens column if you need to."

You have to do things that other people aren't willing to do!

The World Cup. They couldn't have made it – could they?

"Now add up your tens column and don't forget to include any numbers that have been carried over."

The youth of many countries wound up killing each other.

What did the old man mean? Why would athletes kill each other? It didn't make sense.

Although he wasn't particularly focused in lessons, Liam actually enjoyed his day at school. Rather than letting things fester, he surprised Mr James by apologising for his red card the previous afternoon and despite finding his work difficult as usual, he did at least manage to finish it without ripping it to shreds.

Listening to the old man had helped him somehow. He'd had all sorts of difficulties when he was younger and he'd overcome them. His words vibrated in Liam's head – don't be ashamed of who you are.

As soon as the bell rang at the end of the school day, Liam rushed straight home, his eyes glowing with excitement. He bypassed his own house and arrived breathless at the old man's doorstep. He took a minute to compose himself, for after all he didn't want to appear nosey, before ringing the door bell.

It wasn't long before Liam was sat in the same armchair,

watching the old man potter about in the kitchen again. After what seemed like an eternity, he reappeared with a tray.

"One hot chocolate for you sir and a generous amount of custard creams. I'm afraid we're out of jammy dodgers for the time being. Oh - and would sir please ensure he finishes his drink today and doesn't let it get cold."

Liam smiled and studied the plate of biscuits.

"Would sir also please ensure he leaves some custard creams for the other guests."

Liam laughed and settled for just two biscuits.

"I wasn't sure if you'd come back," the old man said, settling into his chair. "Wasn't sure if you'd got bored with me prattling on about how life was back in the day."

Liam could contain himself no longer. He had to ask. "Did you and Stan make it to the first team at Sunderland?"

The old man took a sip of his hot chocolate.

"We did," he replied. "For a while at least. But – yes, we did make it for short time."

Liam was a little confused and maybe even a little disappointed. They'd made it for a while. He'd rather hoped they'd become the star players – even gone on to play for England.

Yes – Liam was disappointed, although he tried hard not to show it. He remained silent for a moment.

"Yesterday", he said eventually. "What did you mean about the youths of many countries winding up killing each other? Did I hear you right?"

The old man's eyes betrayed a certain sadness but his

voice remained calm.

"I can tell you what happened Liam but it's not always a smooth ride. Are you sure you want to know?"

Liam looked across at the photographs on the windowsill and the two smiling youths in their football kits. "I do," he replied.

Chapter 9

Well - by the time I made my debut for Sunderland on an icy-cold winter's day in 1938, they were the FA cup holders. Stan, at the tender age of eighteen had been in the team for three months now and was becoming established as a first team regular. I remember the game as if it were yesterday.

Stan was made up that I'd made the starting line-up. I think it was the most I'd ever seen him speak and he talked my ear off on the way to the ground. He was even more pleased than I was. Stan was so calm and quiet normally that it made me laugh to see him so tense when it was my debut and not his.

"I knew you'd make it Jim," he said, his face a picture of excitement. "I knew the boss would see sense and pick you sooner or later. You'll be a first team-regular in no time.

"Relax Stan," I said. "One step at a time – you're going to make me a nervous wreck in a minute.

He took that in for a moment before replying.

"Well don't play too well. If you make captain before me, I'm not taking orders off you."

We both laughed and for a young lad playing their first game, I was strangely relaxed.

When I arrived at Roker Park, just after twelve o'clock, my kit was laid out neatly for me in the dressing room. Young players these days would normally be introduced from the bench if it was their debut but there were no such things as substitutes in those days so I was being thrown in at the deep end. Sitting in the changing room, I looked like a boy amongst men, with my skinny, chicken legs. My muscles had not fully developed yet and it would be a few years before hard graft in the weights room would drastically alter my physique. That and lung-burning sessions from our coach Paul. He was in charge of the team's physical conditioning. We used to hate him for it at the time but he was a good lad really.

The atmosphere was electric when we ran out before kick-off against Arsenal FC and I got a great reception from our fans. The whole stadium seemed to shake and a sea of red and white scarves flowed through it. A spiteful breeze nibbled at my legs but the famous Roker Park roar made me feel I could run through walls. I felt that I had arrived as a player at last but I was also aware that I had an awful lot to prove. I'd learnt to control my nerves over the last three years and playing reserve team football had toughened me up mentally. I was ready to show people what I could do. Stan had a word with me before we kicked off but I didn't need anyone's help that day. I felt totally focused.

I began the match playing on the left flank and within the opening five minutes, I was given the traditional welcome afforded to youngsters with a bit of speed and skill. I believe they call it the reducer these days. Anyway, the opposition full back's tackle almost cut me in two. If it hadn't taken place on a football pitch, I think he could probably have been arrested for causing grievous bodily harm. It stung for a few minutes but I didn't let it bother me. In fact I told the full back this myself when he was marking me at a corner. I had learnt to stand up for myself during my time in the North-East reserve leagues. I still remember his face when I informed him that his tackles could do with a bit more bite!

I'd already given the Arsenal defence a brief glimpse of my speed with a lightning burst down the touchline, when a few minutes later, I found myself in space about ten yards outside the box. I skipped past the wild, desperate lunge of one opponent, before bursting right between their two centre halves and into the penalty area. Pressurised into a mistake, the full back tried to cover but found himself making an unwise, last ditch attempt to slide in and block my shot. Clipping my ankles, he sent me tumbling to the floor and the crowd erupted, imploring the ref to give the penalty. Despite the outrageous accusations from Arsenal's players, that I had dived, he pointed to the spot.

Defying the attempts of the goalkeeper to put him off, our centre forward rolled the ball casually into the bottom corner, sending the crowd wild. It was absolutely exhilarating. My adrenalin began to flow and I felt absolutely invincible. Encouraged by fifty thousand, screaming voices, I played the game of my life, even winning a few tackles which wasn't really my game.

As the game inched towards half-time, the ball broke to me thirty yards from goal. Usually I would have taken the safe, sensible option and taken a touch before laying it off. However, brimming with confidence, I decided to take it first time. Although it wasn't the purest strike I'd ever hit, it was at an awkward height for the goalkeeper and took a horrendous bobble just in front of him. I watched as it thudded into his chest and evaded his grasp. Stan was on hand to tap the rebound over the line and it was two-nil. As my team-mates embraced me, I knew I was here to stay.

Ten minutes before the end, I scored my first goal for Sunderland. After a glorious triangular passing movement in midfield, Stan played a slide rule pass into space. I was on it in a flash, drifting past defenders whose resistance was fading towards the end of the game and firing the sweetest of shots into the bottom corner. The crowd sang my name long after the final whistle had blown. My debut had been a resounding success and the dream of lifting the World Cup for England didn't seem to be so far away any more.

Chapter 10

Over the next season and a half, I established myself in the Sunderland first team and I was one of the most exciting prospects in England's top division. I was even given a pay rise to the princely sum of £1 a week. Naturally, as with all young players, my form dipped from time to time and I even endured a short spell back in the reserves at one point. I was now a resilient character though and a setback such as this didn't hold me back for long.

I finished the 1938 season as second top scorer with fifteen league goals and despite the club's poor form during the following season, I managed to bag thirteen more. This was a good return considering I had spent three months on the sidelines with a broken bone in my foot. As the new season approached in August 1939, sitting in his parent's kitchen, Stan and I discussed our chances of making the next England squad. If we started the season well, both of us were thought to have a chance of making it.

"Did you ever think we'd make it this far Stan," I asked, sipping a cool glass of ginger ale.

"Never a doubt Jim. Not for a minute. The first time I saw you, I knew you'd play for England. That muscular physique of yours was a giveaway."

"Sarcastic beggar," I laughed, punching him lightly on the arm.

He leant back in his chair, his face a beaming smile. Then he turned serious for a second.

"You were always tougher than you looked you know. At first sight, you don't look like you could blow out a candle but you've got a fire in your belly alright. Hand on heart, I never thought either of us would make it this far but if you don't believe in your dreams who else is ever going to."

I took another gulp of ginger ale. "Hey – do you remember hitting dustbin lids in your back yard when we were training for the semi-finals."

"Like it was yesterday. Hit some of my best shots in that back yard," he replied, grinning at the memory.

"Try telling Mrs Gregory's window that," I said, stifling a laugh. "She was still finding shards of glass in her back garden for three months after your last free kick. It's no wonder the boss doesn't let you take penalties."

"You know how to hurt me," Stan replied shaking his head. "Besides you don't get off scot free. If you'd put a bit more practice in, perhaps you wouldn't have given the keeper a chance in the youth cup semi final."

"OK then. You want a shot at the title," I said, picking up a football from the corner of the room. Penalty shoot out in the back yard. Five shots each then sudden death. Loser does your mum's dishes for her."

"You're on. Let's hope the pressure doesn't get to you."

We were like two immature school kids in the back yard. Deliberately putting each other off and celebrating goals wildly, we competed like it was the World Cup final. I'm sorry to say that Stan won in a sudden death shoot out and proceeded to complete a victory dance around the yard. He had always handled pressure well. In shame and humiliation, I headed to the kitchen sink...

Anyway, when the season finally started, Stan and I were on fire. In the first match, I netted twice, including a spectacular, swerving effort from long range against the champions Everton and in the following away game against Derby County, I added another, sliding the ball in from close range. Stan even rolled in a penalty five minutes from time to secure a three-one win. I never thought I'd hear the end of it after the boss selected him as penalty taker for the season. The papers began to report that the select committee in charge of picking the England squad were giving serious thought of giving us both our first caps. I felt indestructible and that nothing could stop me, but four days later, on Sunday 3rd September came the bombshell that would change my life forever. England's Prime minister, Neville Chamberlain, had declared war on Adolf Hitler's Nazi Germany.

Chapter 11

To be honest with you Liam, the war had come as no surprise really. The previous year had been one of unbearable tension as politicians bluffed and threatened each other. I suppose I was just caught up in my own little football bubble to worry too much about it. Anyhow, on Friday 1st September 1939, Germany had invaded Poland. In the previous year and a half they had overcome Austria and Czechoslovakia. Britain had vowed to assist Poland if Hitler chose to invade, but he had ignored this warning and one million Nazi troops were sent over the border.

It was awful Liam. A cloud seemed to hang across the country. Cricket matches were cancelled, theatres were closed and even greyhound tracks were shut down, but football stumbled on for one more day. The public didn't quite know what to do and neither did we footballers. So, On Saturday 2nd September, the final league games of the 1939-1940 season were played. The atmosphere in every stadium across the country was strange to say the least. Crowds of 70,000 were replaced by those of 8,000 and spectators were in no mood for celebrations even if their team had won. Barrage balloons, to disrupt any falling bombs, were even spotted drifting ominously above Maine Road.

Apparently, there was an especially subdued atmosphere at Arsenal's match in London as the first of the capital's children were evacuated to the countryside. I remember the photographs in the papers of parents refusing to watch as weeping children in carriages left the train stations. Some of those poor kids never saw their parents again Liam. It was just a dreadful time. For once, the result of a football match was not important to me and no more league matches would be played for seven long years.

The following day Stan and I gathered around the kitchen table at his parent's house. Like most families in the UK we were listening to the radio. The announcement came from Neville Chamberlain at 11:15am. His opening words will remain with me until my dying day.

"I am speaking to you from the cabinet room at 10 Downing Street".

He talked gravely about his failure to win peace for the nation and the calmness and courage that would be required from the British public. We were stunned into silence and gripped by a shared sense of dread.

So, over the next week the suspension of the football league was announced as it wasn't considered safe to have large crowds gather during times of war. It wasn't really a great shock but it still left me feeling numb. I knew I was being selfish because there were greater things to worry about than my sporting career but I'd be lying if I didn't admit to shedding a few self pitying tears.

Anyway, it was funny really because Stan and I had spent the last ten years dreaming of our country calling upon us and now they had. All males between eighteen and forty-one who didn't have a particular job such as dock workers or scientists for example, were required to do National Service and fight. Our dreams were in tatters.

Well, being called up by the forces was inevitable for

young lads of our age anyway so Stan and I registered later that month. Men who signed up early were able to choose between the army, the navy or the air force. Stan, perhaps trying to confront his fear of flying head on, insisted that we join the RAF. I wasn't going to argue with him. I'd always wanted to fly in a plane, although I wasn't quite so keen when Stan helpfully pointed out that the Germans would be shooting at us! We were to be given eight months of training. Of course, I didn't know at the time that this was usually a two year course but due to the likely deaths of thousands of airman, the air force would need to rush through more recruits. The RAF bosses must have left that part out of the advertising brochure.

In case you were wondering, we weren't the only footballers in this position. Of the thirty five players on the staff of our rivals, Bolton Wanderers, thirty-two joined the armed services. In fact, reports after the war stated that over six hundred professional footballers joined up. Anyhow, it was eventually decided that we would be posted to the Padgate RAF base in Blackpool for our initial training.

It was January 1940 when my mother and I made the short journey to Stan's parents' house, gathering on the steps for a final photograph. We had received the order to join up and were due to leave the following month. We found ourselves in the kitchen drinking ginger ale again. It had seemed a lifetime ago since we had been in this very spot, plotting our way to an England call-up.

"Well this is it," said Stan, picking at the skin surrounding his nails.

I wasn't used to seeing him like this. He had always taken everything in his stride and never let anything get him down. Now, although his voice remained calm, I could tell he was agitated and his face was pale. I had so much to say but the words were trapped in my throat.

"We'll both get through this you know Jim," he continued. "The war should only last a year and then we can get back out on the pitch. At least the forces will keep us in shape and we won't lose our fitness." I nodded and managed a smile but there was a lump in my throat and a knot in my stomach. There was a long dreadful silence.

"I'm scared Stan," I finally admitted.

There seemed so much more to say but neither of us spoke. When Stan's father Malcolm embraced him, I could see him shaking uncontrollably. It upset me more than I let on as I think it brought home to me the enormity of our circumstances. Anyway, before long, the taxi arrived and his mother gave us both a lingering hug. She'd already seen her older son Jack leave the family home to sign up for the army and I think that seeing Stan leave too was almost too much to bear.

"You promise me you'll look after him," his mother said, wiping her eyes. "You keep my boy safe. Promise me Jim."

"I promise," I replied, but I couldn't look her in the eye.

As for my mother, her tears just wouldn't stop flowing. She hadn't always been easy to live with but I also knew how much warmth and love she had for me. I wanted to find the words to bring her some sort of comfort but I couldn't. I don't think there was anything I could have said that would have eased her hurt. I settled for kissing her tenderly on the cheek. I didn't look back as we pulled away. I think I would have broken down myself.

Chapter 12

When we eventually began our RAF training, nothing much had happened in terms of any serious conflicts. It was believed that Hitler was still considering peace talks. This period was later named the 'phoney war'. In fact, many evacuated children who had gone to stay in the countryside to escape Hitler's bombs, had now returned to their families, not entirely sure of what the fuss had been about.

However, I do recall the war claiming its first victim of the football community when Jack Lambert of Arsenal was killed in a car crash. This was mainly due to the 'blackout' rules that allowed no lights on the streets, houses or even cigarettes after dark. Well, of course, this resulted in almost double the cases of road accidents, leading one hospital surgeon to comment that Hitler was able to kill six hundred British citizens a month without his bombers lifting a finger. I must admit that I did feel he had a point at the time.

Anyway, after an initial meeting with a selection panel and passing a medical that included vision and colour-blindness tests, I had been accepted as a wireless operator while Stan was to be responsible for operating the nose gun and aiming the bombs we would be dropping. He didn't take it too kindly when I mentioned that I hoped he'd have more luck aiming at enemy positions than he did aiming at goalposts. On arrival in Blackpool, we were immediately issued with kit and uniform, along with a civilian suitcase, two kit bags, back pack, side pack and a gas mask case.

On the second day all new recruits had a compulsory haircut. Whether you liked it or not, this would involve electric scissors straight over the top. No comb and scissors would be required and there was certainly no mention of 'what would you like today sir'. As a sign of how much care was put into our appearance, let me tell you that each haircut took ninety seconds. Stan had always been quite proud of his appearance and was horrified to lose his flowing locks.

As part of our initial training, Stan was instructed on how to operate a bomb sight and load and fuse his own missiles, while I worked on the basics of Morse code and was given instructions in how to repair equipment. This could prove vital in the field.

My primary role was to receive messages – we would never give out messages ourselves in case the enemy intercepted them. Every quarter of an hour, there would be a coded transmission from base, which might be information to help the navigator, or I might be told that an airfield had been put out of action and the plane would have to land somewhere else. I would also have to tune in to beacons which transmitted signals to help locate the plane's position and keep checking the rear gunner to make sure he was alright.

In addition to the technical stuff, we were given physical training that usually took place on the beaches and was often carried out by well known sportsman. As Stan and I were up and coming footballers, we were usually selected as assistants. Many recruits soon found out how unfit they were, but we still excelled in the fitness department and, if I closed my eyes when running along the beaches, for a brief moment I could almost imagine racing down the wing at Roker Park, with blood surging through my veins and the crowd chanting my name.

As the first month of our training passed, we soon discovered that flying in a bomber was a lot different to watching one from the ground. I still remember very clearly the first time Stan and I went on a training flight. It always makes me chuckle.

Picture the scene Liam. There's five of us raw recruits waiting nervously on the runway beside our bomber, ready to be taken up into the skies for the first time by two experienced instructors. Don't forget that air travel wasn't so common in those days and none of us had seen the inside of a plane before. Our pilot, Captain Walters, was a somewhat legendary figure in the RAF. He was a large bear of a man, probably in his late forties, with a craggy face and narrow eyes that always appeared to be scrutinising you for some sort of fault in your appearance. Walters had absolutely no time for recruits who were struggling and exchanges with him would be brief and to the point. Basically Liam, if you weren't shaping up to his standards, he wouldn't take long to let you know. I'm probably making him sound like an ogre but he was actually thought of fondly by recruits. He had a razor sharp wit that would often leave us in stitches and his gruff demeanour was softened by a slight clumsiness that often led to him stumbling or tripping. When I think of it, it was a good job that he could control a plane better than he could control his feet.

Well, Walters was a stickler for punctuality and was fuming that one recruit was late for his first training flight.

"Where's Whiteside?" he barked in his familiar Yorkshire tone, not even attempting to hide his exasperation.

As no response was forthcoming, he turned his attention towards me.

"You, Evans. You two are as thick as thieves. Where is he? This won't do."

At that moment Stan appeared. He looked ghostly pale, with wide eyes and jelly-like legs.

For once, Walters was actually lost for words. It must have been a full minute before he spoke.

"And this is a professional athlete," he said to no-one in particular. "This is what those young kiddies in Sunderland look up to is it? Hitler would kill himself laughing if he knew this was the best the RAF could do."

"I'm sorry Sir," Stan muttered softly, "It's just…"

The rest of us immediately lowered our eyes to the ground. It was best to just let Walters blow off steam once he had started. It didn't pay to interrupt him.

"Just what Whiteside! Just what! Speak up boy."

Stan was staring at the bomber, unable to disguise his fear.

"It's just that – well – it's like a giant coffin sir."

Again, Walters was stunned into a momentary silence. He walked right up to Stan – almost nose to nose."

"Footballers," he said, shaking his head sadly. "Bloody

footballers."

He turned on his heels and headed to the plane just a split second before Stan vomited on the floor. Walters had avoided a direct hit but his shiny, pristine shoes would need a touch of polish. His face was a picture.

It's funny really, because once we were airborne, Stan actually felt much better. He was probably the calmest out of all of the recruits and never suffered from pre-flight nerves again. In fact, over the next few months and to my surprise, he even managed to persuade a few of the friendlier pilots who took us up to let him sit up front and watch how to control the plane's flight. That's more than can be said of me I'm afraid. Once we were up there, flying along at ten thousand feet, I felt as sick as a dog and my legs lost all their strength. I think I held on to my seat so tightly that my fingers went numb!

But anyway Liam, I think Stan and I would have felt even more uncomfortable if we had known then that over eight thousand British air force recruits would die without even experiencing enemy combat due to training incidents. I shudder now even as I think of this. You see Liam, back then, in the early 1940s planes were often plagued with mechanical difficulties and staying airborne during a training flight was no foregone conclusion. It wasn't completely unheard of for the tail of a bomber to drop off mid-air! Accidents occurred frequently and with deadly repercussions. I recall one story, told by a fellow recruit of a plane going down in a field in Yorkshire. The crew inside never stood a chance and apparently their mangled bodies couldn't even be recognised. As you can imagine, this didn't do much for my anxiety levels. I began to think that perhaps Stan had been right about flying all along.

The air force did its best to teach us recruits how to survive a crash. We were drilled in impact positions and even for post-crash survival. Perhaps the most terrifying was imagining an emergency landing at sea. It didn't seem like the odds would be with us if this happened. Controlled landings on water seemed virtually impossible. Besides – I'm a terrible swimmer.

So anyhow, one morning, about three months after our arrival at Padgate, Stan and I were enjoying a hearty breakfast at our RAF digs when the postman arrived on his bicycle. He whistled cheerfully as he avoided the playful lunge of our landlady's greyhound and glided across the path to the door. The letter remained stuck for a minute, before drifting to the floor. I recognised the writing. It was from Stan's father. As he opened it, I was alarmed to see his face cloud over with horror.

Chapter 13

Liam sat in his chair speechless. His throat felt tight and a cold chill of apprehension swept over him. What was the letter about? He was shocked. Going up in a bomber plane sounded horrendous. It must have taken nerves of steel. The old man seemed to cloud over for a while and took a minute to compose himself.

"Excuse me for a minute Liam," he said finally. "Sam could do with his water bowl filling up."

With that, he left the room and began pottering about in the kitchen. He was only out of the room for a matter of minutes but to Liam it felt like forever. He could hear the rustling of boxes as if the old man was searching for something.

Finally, he returned carrying the dog's water bowl, an extra couple of custard creams and some sort of cardboard box.

"There you go," he said, handing a biscuit to me. "All that chatting can make a man get hungry." He took the top off the cardboard box and set it on the coffee table. "What do you think of this then Liam?"

Leaning forward and dropping the odd crumb of custard cream, Liam took a look inside. It was an old, red and white football shirt. The fabric was a little worn but it was still in pretty good condition. It certainly didn't look as flashy as today's premier league shirts but Liam was still impressed. In his mind's eye, he imagined the old man in his younger days, celebrating a winning goal in front of adoring fans.

"This was the shirt I wore in my final game before the war started. I suppose I kept it as I wasn't sure if I'd ever play again. Pulling on the red and white stripes made me feel ten feet tall. They were great times."

With a sigh, the old man sat down in his armchair. "Now where was I," he asked. "When you get to my age, you'll find yourself forgetting things sometimes."

"The letter," Liam whispered with a touch of apprehension. "The letter from Stan's father. Was everything OK?"

The old man ran his fingers across his temple and slowly down the sides of his face. He took a deep breath and began to talk.

Do you know Liam, that while Stan and I were training with the RAF, football in the United Kingdom was starting to rise from the ashes. As Britain had not experienced any bombing raids, the Football League even decided to start a new competition entitled the Football League War Cup. The final was actually due to take place in June 1940. I'd be lying if I told you it hadn't crossed my mind that Stan and I could have been there. However, by the time the final took place, the 'Phoney War' had ended and for Stan the reality of war had struck close to home. His older brother Jack, who Stan absolutely idolised, had been badly wounded and it was touch and go whether he'd survive.

Jack wasn't a battle hardened soldier. He was as tough as old boots but he was just a civilian. Just over two months earlier, he had been helping Stan's father manage their Greengrocers business and now he was lying in a hospital bed. Seventy days – that's all the time he was given to acquire the skills to fight for his country, learning how to fire many types of weapon such as rifles, shotguns and pistols. He learnt how to plant mines, throw grenades and dig trenches to build defence positions before being called up to join the British forces in France and prevent the Germans from advancing. Imagine it Liam – seventy days. To me, it didn't seem any time at all for young men like Jack to prepare for war.

Well anyway, towards the end of spring in 1940, Jack had been one of approximately 400,000 men, cornered by Hitler's rampaging army at the port of Dunkirk in Northern France. The papers were full of the story. In a desperate attempt at an unlikely rescue, an unbelievable armada had set sail from the shores of Britain. Yachts, ferries, motorboats, fishing boats, barges and just about every other type of vessel you could possibly think of sailed across the channel. Each boat was manned by only one or two everyday people such as bankers, dentists and taxi drivers. In pitch-black darkness, they left the English coast, making a huge traffic lane of ghostly, silhouetted shapes.

Guided by a fire storm of smoke and flames they approached the beaches through treacherous waters, trying their best to avoid bombs from German planes. In the distance, the beaches were clogged with retreating soldiers. If they were not rescued, the war would already be lost. Lines of soldiers staggered across sandy dunes and into the sea while shells splashed into the water, cutting down men as they tried to make their escape. Smaller boats ferried the luckier ones to larger ships as they waited in deeper water. The noise was ear-splitting, with never-ending machine gun fire and snarling plane engines roaring through plumes of towering smoke. The town glowed a fiery red in the background.

Well, over the next seven days, streams of exhausted soldiers continued to make their way to safety. The discipline of the men was amazing. For three long weeks, they had retreated through France, often without sleep, food or water. Despite the chaos surrounding them, they kept rank as they came down the beaches and obeyed the commands they were given.

Despite the huge amount of vehicles and weapons left behind, the evacuation saved the lives of hundreds of thousands of British, French and Belgian troops. Many high ranking military commanders had been saved too and the British people considered it a major success in the fight against Germany.

However, over 60,000 men had been killed or captured. Badly wounded, and one of the last soldiers to be evacuated, Stan's brother Jack had watched the carnage fade while his boat moved gradually away from Dunkirk. Beside burned out ships, charred lorries and rotting horses lay thousands of corpses. He had a fleeting moment of guilt about the brave soldiers that had been left behind, keeping the Germans at bay for long enough that others could escape. Then he passed out.

Shortly after the final evacuations from Dunkirk, Stan took a train to London to visit Jack in hospital. He found him lying in bed asleep, his body savaged by bullets and shrapnel. He had been shot in the upper arm, the chest and one bullet had grazed the side of his head. Most horrifically of all, doctors had needed to amputate his left leg below the knee. He'd live but his injuries were life changing. I know it hit Stan hard. Jack was a tough as they come and to Stan he'd always seemed invincible. Seeing his older brother, his hero, lying there with his body broken, was a sight he would never forget. The British papers may have painted Dunkirk as a victory, but to those of us in the forces, it was a wake-up call. The war would not be over in a year. The Germans were well organised, armed with advanced weaponry and weren't going to go away. This would be the battle of our generation.

Chapter 14

So it must have been August 1940 when the initial period of our training was over and both Stan and I passed with excellent grades. I had achieved 90% on my theory test and 85% when operating in the air. To my immense pride, I had become a sergeant wireless operator. We would now be posted to Lincoln to prepare for flying heavy bombers on vital missions. We were assigned to a crew that would be ready for operational missions within three months.

During this time, Stan and I became friendly with another trainee in the group. Mick Brayson was a twenty-one year old from Leeds and was a rear gunner. We hit it off immediately and shared similar interests and abilities. He had followed our football careers with interest and would often grill us for inside information about men I had played with or against. Mick was such an upbeat character that he was able to raise your spirits and drag you out of a slump whenever things got too much.

Besides Mick, Stan and I, our crew consisted of three others. Serving as our pilot would be Fred Taylor, a friendly self assured young man from Newcastle. Tempting as it was, you'll be pleased to know that I didn't hold this against him. Operating as waist gunner and observer would be Henry Mitchell who originated from Merseyside. He was a keen football fan and would always be goading me by telling me about his beloved Everton. Of course, Stan would be on the nose gun, while doubling up as bomb aimer, which just left the loud but loveable Jonny Morris from Manchester who was the flight engineer and navigator. Good looking and charming, he could talk you to death given half a chance.

We would be flying in a Wellington Bomber, a long range plane capable of carrying two tons of bombs. I had secretly been hoping for the faster Mosquito model as it had a far better record in terms of keeping its inhabitants in the air. This is quite an important attribute I'm sure you'd agree. In fact, it wouldn't be too long before Wellingtons were phased out of bombing raids as more advanced models replaced them as the war progressed. However, for now we had to make do and get on with the job in hand.

For the next few months, we practically lived in the plane, often completing exhausting ten hour training flights. Flying in formation with other bombers, we fired at targets towed by other planes, simulated combat runs and practised dive bombing. We had a few scares, including getting lost and only just making it back to base before our fuel ran out. This was not something to take lightly as, like I mentioned earlier, accidents were frequent and deadly.

Mick, Stan and I were inseparable and tried to keep in good spirits, despite unnerving reports of Germany's progression through Europe and the constant stories of flight crews never returning from training runs. We went running together to maintain physical fitness, danced with young ladies at parties and Mick even showed us the finer arts of spin bowling. Cricket was one of his favourite hobbies.

Playing pranks on the rest of the crew was one of Mick's ways to lighten the mood. One of his favourite tricks was to drizzle honey over any unsuspecting member of the crew who was unfortunate enough to take a snooze at the base. Of course, when you awoke to this strange sensation, the first reaction was to wipe a hand over your face. From first-hand experience of this, I can tell you that this soon becomes a very sticky situation.

Another of his favourite jokes was to make you flood the barracks bathroom. Filling a garbage can about three quarters full with water, he would lean it up against the door, before escaping out of the window. From a nearby vantage point, he would then sit back and watch a victim open the door and completely flood the room.

I still remember the fun Mick got out of Stan. He was the most gullible of all the air crew and therefore a prime target for pranks. One time Mick bet Stan that he couldn't roll a silver three-pence coin down the middle of his nose and then catch it. After Stan had taken several attempts, he finally cracked it, whooping with delight. Little did he know that Mick had carefully traced the outside of the coin with a pencil over and over again. Stan was now walking around with a long black strip of lead on his face. The rest of us were in stitches!

Anyhow moving on, to our delight, Stan and I even had a brief revival of our football careers. As I mentioned a little earlier, although official leagues had been suspended, football was grinding on slowly, regardless of the chaos that had enveloped Europe. I think it was good for the morale of the public more than anything else. Football is after all the people's game in England. Winston Churchill said as much himself!

Anyway, our footballing rebirth came about through an exhibition match between an FA select team and an RAF eleven. It was great to get my boots back on and although I was a rusty, I did manage to score during a 4-2 defeat, latching on to a great pass from Stan, rounding their keeper and rolling the ball into the net. Naturally, we celebrated as if I'd scored the winning goal in the FA cup final and for those brief moments we didn't have care in the world. Ninety minutes of football was an escape from the realities of war and allowed me the faintest glimmer of hope that one day I'd resume my career. Stan was in no doubt whatsoever. Perhaps getting a little carried away, he was already talking about how the Sunderland team would line up next season.

Chapter 15

Well, anyway, while we continued with our training, over the skies of London, just after 4pm in early September, residents began to hear a low droning getting progressively louder. Two hours later the city was ablaze. Apparently, there had been over 600 fighter planes supporting another three hundred or so German bombers as they unleashed a fearsome assault on the capital. The Blitz had begun.

The next day, Stan and I studied the papers in horror. Lots of the other boys had relatives who lived in London and were desperate to hear updates on their safety. The first wave of bombings had lasted for two ferocious hours and just as residents drew breath, a further group of raiders, guided by the fires, began another attack that hadn't stopped until 4.30 the next morning. We were aghast! The whole country was aghast!

The bombing campaign against London was relentless. For fifty-seven consecutive nights sirens wailed out their warnings across the city and remorseless fires savaged their way through housing areas. During breaks in my training, I listened to the wireless as eye-witnesses told of brave fire-fighters doing battle with crackling flames, buildings being ripped apart and planes buzzing overhead like angry wasps. Everyone at the base was on edge and sick with worry.

Of course London wasn't the only British city to suffer,

and soon enough the streets of Liverpool, Cardiff and Southampton, to name a few, would be set on fire and covered in suffocating smoke. One devastating night in Coventry saw the biggest air-raid the world had ever witnessed. Thousands of homes were destroyed and hundreds of people killed. Apparently, at one point during the night 200 separate fires burned in the city. Ultimately, over 30,000 people would lose their lives in the Blitz. My heart went out to their families. Even football stadiums that I had played at did not escape the barrage. The ten bombs that hit Sheffield United's Bramall Lane ground demolished half the John Street Stand and badly damaged the pitch.

So, towards the end of 1940, a battle for national survival had been raging in the skies above Britain for a few months now. This struggle would decide the future of the country and the freedom of Europe. We young men who made up air crews would suddenly become the front line of defence for the entire nation. Those of us in Bomber Command would be given the task of hitting strategic targets in Germany or other parts of occupied Europe while Fighter Command would attempt to prevent the enemy from aerial attacks.

You see Liam, Fighter Command airmen would have a very different role from those of us in Bomber Command. They would fly in short range, faster planes such as Spitfires and Hurricanes. These aircraft could reach top speeds of over 550kph and were way more mobile than our Wellington Bombers. They didn't have a six man crew – just a pilot on his own.

Britain was now on its own. Our close allies France

had surrendered during the summer and Hitler's Panzer tanks were sweeping through all opposition in Europe. The Netherlands and Belgium had already been defeated. Cities such as Rotterdam had been bombed without mercy by German planes. Thousands of innocent people had been killed and many more had been left homeless. Hitler had even been photographed in front of the Eiffel Tower, declaring to the world he was the master of Europe and only Britain stood in his way. There was talk of an imminent, full scale invasion against our country being ordered and we had to fight back. For Stan and I, the time had come. This was it.

Chapter 16

Our crew had been selected to form part of a bombing raid on Gelsenkirchen in the Ruhr region of Germany. The plan was to strike at the industrial sites that made aviation fuel. This was a priority for the RAF. Do you know Liam, that this was to be the first of a possible thirty missions that Stan and I were supposed to fly. After that our first tour of duty would be done. Doesn't seem so bad does it? Well – it didn't feel so good when you knew that only one in four airmen would live through those thirty missions. If I was lucky enough to live through my first tour, I'd be given a six month break before completing a second tour. If by some miracle that I survived this too, I'd be done. You can see why we airmen didn't think too far ahead and lived life day by day.

Well, in the days leading up to that first mission, I have to admit that I was incredibly tense. There was no escaping the fact that flying in a British Bomber was one of the most dangerous jobs imaginable. Raids over German positions were often disastrous as our planes were slow and lumbering, making for easy targets. Many planes never made it back. For us it was almost impossible to dismiss the risks involved. Dead airmen weren't just numbers in a newspaper story, for us, they were room-mates, friends or people who had been flying next to us the previous day.

There were times when I felt like I was surrounded by death. When you lost a friend, you couldn't even say goodbye to them properly as there were rarely funerals. I'd be lying if I said I wasn't afraid. We all were – Stan, Mick and even Jonny Morris who didn't normally have a care in the world. I remember sitting with Stan on the steps outside our digs the day before the first mission. I was on edge and even Stan was struggling to find reasons for optimism.

"Do you think we'll be alright Jim," said Stan, his eyes looking down at the floor.

He was tense – we'd all heard the horror stories of bomber crews being shot out of the sky. The odds weren't going to be with us. If we weren't going to be hit tomorrow, there was every chance that it would happen sooner or later. I tried to stay strong but I could feel my voice breaking as I spoke. I tried not to show it but I felt sick.

"We'll be alright Stan," I said unconvincingly, "We've all just got to stay sharp, look after each other, and we'll be alright.

"Jim – if I don't make it back – you know – if the worst happens."

"Stan – we can't begin to think like that."

"I know – I know – It's just – I want you to tell my parents that I..."

He couldn't finish his sentence but I knew what he was trying to say. His eyes were distant and misty and I could see the fear in them.

"I'll tell them Stan," I said. "It'll be alright."

Did I think we would be? Let me tell you Liam – I didn't

sleep a wink that night.

So anyway, the next evening, our crew of six boarded our Wellington bomber, joining forty other planes that would carry out the raid on the Ruhr. Although it must have taken two or three hours to reach Germany, I don't think there were more than a few words spoken during the entire journey. I tried not to show it to the other boys but I can tell you I was scared stiff. There was a threatening silence hanging in the air – a sort of calm before the storm to come and the six of us would scan the skies anxiously for signs of enemy defenders. Despite my heavy flak suit and gloves and steel helmet, I shivered continually. The planes had no heating and the temperature could drop rapidly. I think my teeth must have chattered the entire way.

The silence was finally broken as Jonny informed us that we were fifteen minutes from our target destination. We started to spot some flak but it was a long way below us. In fact, it seemed rather beautiful at first, with different coloured puffs of smoke, lighting up the world below us. It was almost like watching a wonderful firework show as we glided along without so much as a ripple.

Then, without warning, an ear-splitting burst of sound rocked the sky. Furious explosions of colour streaked towards us and flak whistled through the air from above and below. Something struck the right hand side of the plane and it sank momentarily. I couldn't help letting out a gasp of horror and almost instantly, I saw the bomber to our right take a hit and drop away sharply before disappearing below us. It passed us so closely that I could see the faces of the men inside. I tried to keep my focus, although I couldn't help thinking about those aboard the stricken plane. They would surely die!

Meanwhile, Stan was focused on the task of dropping the bombs we were carrying onto the targets below. As he took aim and prepared to release the first batch, our plane was rocked by a shuddering crash. A shell had knocked off a part of the rudder about the size of a snooker table. For a moment, Stan was disorientated but recovered quickly enough to get his bombs away. They dropped down, spinning towards their targets. A slight hammer of guilt hit me as I thought of the destruction they would wreak below. I prayed that they would hit their targets and no civilians would be hurt.

Well, anyhow, Stan managed to get two more batches away and we could see towering clouds of smoke appear below us. However, there was no time to observe the damage. Fifty or so German fighters were suddenly buzzing around us, sending bursts of machine gun fire into the side of our plane. I saw another three of our bombers suddenly blow up and drop right out of the sky. Others, under heavy fire, began to slip out of formation and were hounded by the German planes. It was like being part of a disaster movie. That's what it felt like at the time.

Then suddenly, screaming in from somewhere, a cannon shell exploded onto the waist of our plane. The bomber lurched violently and it felt like everything had been tipped on its side. A piece of shrapnel must have gone right through my suit and struck my upper arm. I could feel it burning into me but there wasn't time to feel sorry for myself. I could hear the anxiety in Stan's voice coming through the radio from his position on the nose gun.

"Everyone alright back there. Everyone alright."

Well Liam, bullets continued to rip through the body of the plane and I could see the sky through visible holes that had been torn by the machine guns. Every few seconds that passed, the holes seemed to grow in number and I could feel bullets slicing through the air.

Another shell hit the side of the plane and it rocked and shuddered. To be honest with you Liam, I thought that was it. Everything seemed to slow down for a moment just like it had in the cup semi final many years before. The blast must have knocked out inter-phone connections because I'd lost radio contact. The plane was badly damaged but somehow it limped onwards like some sort of stricken animal refusing to give up its fight for life.

Grabbing a first aid kit, I crawled towards the back of the plane, wondering if anyone else had been hurt. As I approached the mid-section, I saw Henry Mitchell clinging to his gun tightly in the turret above me, blood gushing from a deep wound on his leg, where shrapnel had embedded itself. His trouser legs had been torn to shreds and he wore a pained expression on his face. A large jagged hole about the size of a football had been torn in the side of the plane. I moved towards him to tend to his injuries but he ushered me away. He wouldn't leave his gun and continued to fire away at the German planes following us.

Amid the roar of relentless machine gun fire, I moved

unsteadily. The next moments will stay with me forever. I can promise you that. Well, when I reached the rear of the plane, I saw Mick and my heart sank. He had made it out of the turret but was slumped against the fuselage wall. His eyes were bulging out of their sockets and his upper body was soaked with blood. On closer inspection, I could see gaping holes that had punctured his jacket and the back of his hair was crimson red. He was conscious but hurt badly. As I reached out to take hold of him, he fell towards me and I only just about managed to hold him upright. He tried to say something but his words were strained and incoherent and when I eventually managed to sit him down, he passed out.

Trying desperately to ignore a paralysing fear that seemed to have control over my body, I strapped an oxygen mask over Mick's face and bandaged his head. I gave him a shot of morphine and sprinkled the wounds on his back with sulfa powder. There wasn't much more I could do but hope. Reluctantly leaving Mick's side, I took over his position on the tail gun, firing away until it jammed. Stan and Henry continued to pound away at the German fighters and, after what seemed an eternity, they began to slacken off. They must have chased us for about forty minutes before they finally gave up.

It turned out that one of our engines had been completely shot out and we flew so slowly that we lost our place in the formation. We flew virtually alone over France before seeing four fighters in the distance. Everyone thought we were done for but it turns out they were ours. It was an incredible relief and we were able to limp our way to the channel in relative safety. However, none of us really felt like celebrating.

The injured Henry Mitchell had finally left his gun and was sat next to Mick on the floor while Stan had left the nose gun to help tend to his wounds. Henry's leg had pretty much been torn to pieces but he'd live. Mick had come off worse. I could hardly bare the sound of his rasping breath as I knelt beside him. On a few occasions, he opened his eyes briefly and tried to whisper something in my ear but I couldn't work out what he was trying to say. He would then drift off again for lengthy periods. I felt sure he was dying but I kept my thoughts to myself. When I caught Stan's eye, I knew he felt the same.

We finally arrived back in England. The landing was a little bumpy but we had made it. Stan gave the signal that there were wounded men aboard and in seconds we were surrounded by medics rushing Mick away on a stretcher with Henry close behind. As for me, my injured arm was pulsing with pain but I was able to walk to the small infirmary building for treatment. It was about an hour later when Stan told me the awful news that Mick hadn't made it. We were both numb with grief and I'm not ashamed to say that I wept until there were no tears left to shed. Mick was dead. It was just three days before his twenty-second birthday.

Chapter 17

Liam sat in the back of the old man's garden under a cloudless, cheerful sky. It had been three days since he last visited. The two of them were sipping a glass of ginger beer and working themselves through a packet of the old man's endless supply of biscuits.

"Do you still miss Mick?" Liam asked, his voice barely audible.

"Only now and then," the old man replied. "Time is a wonderful healer of even the most painful of wounds. Of course, almost everyone lost someone close to them in the war, be it a great pal or a family member. I wasn't alone in having that dreadful feeling of loss. Mick's parents were devastated and the rest of the crew were shattered too. Mick was such a popular bloke, always making people laugh and keeping spirits up."

The old man stayed silent for a moment, sipping at his ginger beer.

"I suppose there are little things which bring back painful memories," he said at last. "I can't stand watching any of those dreadful hospital dramas on the TV. Watching someone being rushed off a stretcher or pouring with blood takes me back to the inside of that plane."

He paused again and his blue eyes flickered.

"Or cricket," he said. "I find myself watching a test match

and really enjoying it but then I start thinking that Mick would have loved this. Of course after that, I can't bring myself to watch the end. I bet you think I'm stupid really."

"No I don't – I think you're great," Liam blurted out before feeling a sharp pang of embarrassment. He didn't want to sound soppy.

The old man smiled a little to himself. He pulled a manila envelope from his pocket.

"I thought I'd show you this today," he said. "When I was in the barracks hospital recovering, I received a letter from Stan's father. It really cheered me up during that difficult time. I'll read it to you if you like."

Liam nodded his head and the old man began to read the letter.

Dear Jim,

I'm sorry to hear that you have been laid up recently and I hope by the time you receive this you are well and truly on the mend. It would appear that neither you, or either of my boys are particularly skilled at avoiding enemy fire. It's funny really as I never thought that any of you were particularly injury prone before.

Listen Jim, I know you must be in low spirits right now. Stan told me that you'd lost a close pal and there's nothing I can say that will bring him back. I know this sort of thing is awful. Everyone's lost people close to them and I know you all must be hurting. Please find the strength to look to the future as after all, this war can't last forever.

So what's this about you getting your boots on again? Did I really read reports that you'd managed to get a game for the RAF and that you even got on the score sheet? You must still be in pretty good shape. Good job too as Sunderland are going to need you boys on top form for next season. Let's hope that this war is over and done with by the summer so you're ready for kick off. Remember – Jim – I've always thought of you as my third son. I'm counting on you and I'm with you in thoughts if not in person.

Keep your chin up and give the best that's in you. Look after yourself as well as my boy Stan, and I'll see you soon.

Much love as always - Malcolm

The old man put the letter back in the envelope and smiled. Do you know Liam, that for every one of us fighting in the war, letters from friends and family were a godsend. They were a great comfort to you and gave you hope for the future. I don't think we would have defeated the Germans without them as they were a great motivator for the troops. It was important to know that you had people who cared about you and that there was a life to return to one day, no matter distant that seemed. Getting a letter, when it happened, was a delight and I felt much better after hearing from Stan's father. For a moment I tried to believe that perhaps he was right. The war may not last too long and maybe, just maybe, we could get on with our lives again soon. Of course, the sooner the better as far as I was concerned because I had another twenty-nine missions to fly before my active service was complete. Having struggled to get through the first one alive, I wasn't very confident in making double figures, let alone thirty.

Chapter 18

So anyway, my injuries weren't severe enough to keep me out of action for long. I'd lost a bit of blood I suppose, but there was no lasting damage and it was only three weeks later that I flew my second mission to Germany. I was back with my old crew from the fateful bombing of Gelsenkirchen and I was given a warm welcome from Stan, Fred and the rest of the boys. As a result of his injuries Henry had been replaced on the waist gun by Keith Areington, a quiet young lad from Bolton and a new rear gunner named Dennis Wright had replaced Mick. Although, like I said, the boys all seemed pleased to see me, I'd be lying if I said it wasn't a little awkward. Mick had simply been replaced as if he had never existed and of course no-one really talked about it. It wasn't really the thing to speak of when you were preparing for another dangerous mission.

Well, when flying on that second mission, I wasn't really scared at all. Even now, I'm not quite sure why. You'd have thought I'd have been terrified but I wasn't. I think one explanation I could give was that deep down, despite the reassuring words in Malcolm's letter, I don't think I actually believed that I'd live through the war. The horrors of my very first mission haunted me but rather than filling me with fear I was strangely relaxed. I think perhaps that I had come to accept that I would probably die during a bombing raid and didn't feel that desperation to survive.

Do you know Liam, that after the war, I read accounts

from fellow pilots who admitted that their most overwhelming fear had arrived in their final two or three missions. You see, they have more to lose then. They'd got so close to beating the odds against their survival that they were able to see a future beyond the war. This could bring an almost unbearable tension as the final few raids were counted away.

Well, thankfully the second raid didn't go too badly and we all returned safely. In fact, the next six or seven missions passed without too much incident apart from Dennis, the new rear gunner, being wounded by machine gun fire that struck his foot. It didn't seem like any of the 'Tail-end Charlies' had much luck. Unlike Mick, Dennis wasn't too badly wounded though. I still remember the look on his face when I gave him first aid. He seemed more surprised than hurt, almost like a child who's been prevented from playing a game.

Well anyhow, the next four months or so flew past and, somewhat miraculously, Stan and I had completed eleven of the required missions. We'd had a few scrapes along the way but nothing that compared to the first raid on Gelsenkirchen, although our crew now had its third rear gunner, a cocky young man from Yorkshire called Sid. I forget his surname but he was quite a character. Fancied himself as a bit of a ladies' man did Sid although none of us ever saw him have the slightest bit of success with a woman and it wasn't for the want of trying either.

So, as the second half of 1941 approached rapidly, the war raged on. We in Britain stood alone, as Germany and its allies rampaged through the rest of Europe. Then, early that summer, Hitler made a decision that many people felt saved Britain. I suppose we didn't realise it fully at the time. Hitler had decided to invade Russia and directed the might of the German air force to Eastern Europe and away from us. This gave the country valuable breathing space as it had appeared that it was only a matter of time before a German invasion would take place. The Blitz had finally ended.

Well, as Stan and I counted away the missions before reaching the magic number of thirty, life rumbled on. I still wasn't convinced that I'd make the end of my active service in one piece but as the crew completed our fifteenth raid it did seem to all of us that there could be hope. In fact, it was generally considered that the odds of survival would be fifty-fifty for a crew at this stage of a tour of duty. None of us really liked to talk about it that much as we didn't want to tempt fate.

Between missions every member of the crew stayed busy. I think that if you were left alone with your thoughts for too long, your anxieties would overpower you. Stan and I had been crushed by Mick's death, but as I said earlier, losing a friend wasn't uncommon in those days and there was no time to grieve or feel miserable. You had to keep your spirits up or it was impossible to find the strength to go up in those planes and risk your life every week. I suppose all of us lived by the concept of 'Eat drink and be merry, for tomorrow we die'. When given a weekend pass, we'd all head off on wild expeditions to Manchester or even London. This would normally involve consuming considerable quantities of alcohol and flirting with members of the opposite gender. It was all harmless fun really and helped create a bond between us young men. You needed that sense of unity when you were putting your life in each other's hands.

Chapter 19

So, it was towards the end of July 1941, when I flew my eighteenth mission for the RAF. Even though it is such a long time ago the events remain vivid in my memory. I can still recall the propellers whirring lazily as our plane sat on the runway with fifteen other bombers, ready for take-off. We were to take part in an assault on the German city of Frankfurt and to everyone's relief it had gone without a hitch. With job done, I remember discussing breakfast with Stan and the delicious bacon and eggs that awaited us on our safe return. He was always fond of a bacon roll was Stan. That and a coffee laced with a hint of rum to settle the nerves. I think all of us on board were winding down a little to tell you the truth, confident that the mission had been a success. It was stupid really as we all knew that the Germans would have late night fighter squadrons ready to attack from bases in nearby Belgium and the Netherlands.

Well, we must have been just over the Belgian border, when all thoughts of food were suddenly ripped from us as I heard a dreadful sound like a hailstorm on a tin roof. A group of enemy Messerschmitts had caught us by surprise, slamming bullets into our plane's fuselage. I looked to my left and saw that one of the engines was on fire. Flames were now smothering the wing along with one of the fuel tanks and high octane petrol could explode at any time. Up front, Fred and Jonny had obviously seen it too as I heard Fred give the order to feather the engine and switch on the fire extinguisher. Fortunately this worked but we were down to two working engines as the port side one had simply stopped functioning. Obviously, this wasn't great news. We were losing height all the time, leaving us more and more vulnerable to anti-aircraft fire from below. Things hadn't been this perilous since our very first mission.

A further stream of bullets ripped into the aluminium skin of the fuselage and I heard Fred cry out in pain. It turned out that he'd been hit in the left arm but even more worryingly, the plane was not responding to the controls and we were losing even more height. We must have been at no more than 3,000 feet, and through the darkness, I could see the ground below, approaching menacingly. Wincing with pain, Fred gave the order to abandon the aircraft. If we had waited any longer, it would have been too late to use the parachutes anyway.

What happened next moves me every time I think about it. I owe every day that I've lived since that night to my friend Stan. Without his bravery, I wouldn't be here talking to you Liam. You see, to my horror, as we clipped on our parachutes, I found that my harness had been shot off and I'd be unable to jump. I can't even begin to explain how sickening that feeling was.

I was done for. I even contemplated jumping out of the plane without my chute, preferring a quick death to the possible alternative of being burnt alive in a plane wreck.

Well anyhow, I told the rest of the boys the bad news on the intercom and as I glanced over at Stan, he looked horrified. He just sat there and appeared to be frozen with shock. Eventually he managed to mumble a few words, simply telling me that we were in this together and things would be alright. I must admit that I didn't see how they would be. It was a hopeless situation.

There simply wasn't time for any sort of emotional goodbye. Sid went first, jettisoning the escape hatch in the floor, giving a nervous smile and then rolling into the pitch-black darkness. He was swiftly followed by Jonny and Keith, who both knelt by the gaping hatch before disappearing through it. Only Fred, Stan and I remained. The aircraft must have been down to two thousand feet by now.

So, I was sat there in a trance, almost accepting my fate. I remember thinking that Fred and Stan would need to bail out soon or it would be too late. It would be suicide to wait any longer. Then, to my surprise, Stan told me that he was staying with me. It was the bravest thing I'd ever heard. He didn't make a big deal out of it but simply told me that we'd be better off taking our chances with a crash landing.

Fred had let him take control of the Wellington a few times during training flights and Stan felt like he knew enough to give us half a chance of survival on landing. He made it sound like landing the plane was a better option than parachuting out but we both knew this wasn't true. He just didn't have the heart to send me to my death.

"How hard can it be to crash a plane," he joked weakly. I managed to force a nervous smile.

Giving us both a quick handshake and wishing us luck, Fred allowed Stan to take the controls before jumping out of the hatch before it was too late.

Well, the plane kept dropping and I felt in my heart that

we were doomed. I felt numb but managed to move into the brace position that we had rehearsed during flight training. Stan continued to wrestle with the controls, trying to keep the plane level and leave us a fighting chance of survival. We didn't say a further word to each other. I watched the ground race towards us. I wondered what death would feel like and prayed to God that it would be quick and painless. I imagined for one terrible moment the force of the impact and how it would crush us. I had seen enough planes hit the ground and burst into flames. As I held my breath, the seconds passed one at a time.

With an almighty thud, the plane landed on its belly in a large field. We must have struck the ground at around two hundred knots but the plane stayed intact, careering across the grass for what seemed like an eternity. I felt my body being catapulted forwards and my head thumping into the walls of the plane. We hurtled onwards and I closed my eyes, waiting for the inevitable crash and the devastation it would bring. But it never arrived. The plane came to a shuddering halt and there was a moment of stillness and silence.

Smelling petrol fumes and fearing that the plane would erupt at any moment, Stan and I tumbled out from the wreckage and onto the wet grass below. From a safe distance we lay there in the darkness, too stunned to speak. I became acutely aware of a thumping pain to the right of my temple and as I reached out to assess the damage, I felt warm spurts of blood, streaming down my face in thick sheets. I felt my eyes glazing over and the world turned black in front of me.

Chapter 20

I don't know exactly how long I was unconscious for. I was vaguely aware of Stan's voice, urging me to stay with him and in the brief moments that I managed to open my eyes, my head felt like it had been trampled on by an elephant. Despite the mild temperatures at this time of year, I felt unbearably cold and my throat was as dry as a bone. In the distance, I could hear the anti-aircraft guns blasting away mercilessly and I'm sure I heard unfamiliar voices hissing out orders. I wondered if the Germans had found us already and I flicker of fear swept through me. I'd heard a few horror stories of what allied airmen could expect upon capture. I didn't really know if they were true but it frightened me anyway.

The voices around me grew louder still and I became aware that Stan was carrying me over his shoulder. We weren't alone either. I could make out two shadowy shapes alongside us. They seemed to glide effortlessly across the ground and in and out of the cover of trees that lined the track ahead. I could hear Stan breathing heavily from the effort of carrying me and I wondered how far we would be able to go.

Well, the path began to twist and turn before fading away completely and we were soon within a thick forest. Violent shivers continued to attack my weakening body and I couldn't help gripping on tightly to Stan's neck as we stumbled onwards. To my horror, his collar was soaked with blood. It took a few seconds for me to realise that it was mine.

With every step that Stan took, my head pounded relentlessly. Silhouettes of towering trees flickered in front of my eyes and I bit my lip in an attempt to stay awake. My whole body seemed to be begging my eyes to close but I was afraid of blacking out again. I wasn't sure if I'd ever wake up. I could hear faint barking from behind us and I knew the Germans would be searching for us. However, even when they found the downed plane, they would probably presume that everyone had bailed out. With parachutes drifting large distances, this would mean that there could be an area of around 25 square miles for the Germans to search for us.

I was sure I could hear rifle shots in the distance, although I have to say that with the way my head was feeling I couldn't be certain at the time. I did have a brief thought that Fred, Jonny and the rest of the crew may have encountered enemy troops but I pushed this image away as quickly as it had entered my mind.

As Stan lumbered on with me on his shoulders, thin tree branches slashed at my cheeks before breaking in half while leaves crunched on the ground beneath us. We continued to follow the mysterious figures but all of a sudden they stopped dead in their tracks and knelt behind a bramble bush. Stan joined them and set me down momentarily. One of the figures held a finger to his lips and no-one moved a muscle. We waited for a matter of seconds but at the time it felt like an eternity.

Then I heard it. Just faintly at first. Just a gentle pounding. Thud-thud-thud. At first I thought it was my heart hammering through my chest. I lay there in the dark, too weak and afraid to move. I wasn't totally convinced that there was anything there at all but Stan and the other men must have heard something too. Wincing with pain, I managed to sneak a cautious glance around the side of the bramble bush. It was pitch black still. I could see nothing.

Just as the shadowy figures seemed ready to move again, it came again. This time it was closer. Thud-thud-thud. Something was coming towards us, no more than fifty metres or so to our left. I waited, straining to hear any further sound.

The noise was clearer now. Heavy footsteps were coming from what must have been a nearby road and without warning streams of torchlight burst through the trees surrounding us. What little breath I had left remained stuck in my throat and I felt certain that we would be discovered. It was just a matter of time.

Anyway, a patrol of what must have been around a dozen German soldiers passed by, in all likelihood searching for any survivors that had emerged from our stricken plane. We waited and waited for a voice to cry out and signal our discovery but it never came. I guess the good lord felt that we were owed a bit of luck after our plane was shot down. Perhaps he was evening the score. I don't know and I don't really care.

Well, as soon as the coast was clear, Stan hoisted me back up on his shoulders and we were on the move again. The brief rest seemed to have reinvigorated him as he moved almost twice as quickly as before. Perhaps it was a rush of adrenalin after almost being captured. Deeper and deeper into the forest we went, wading through a wide stream on the way.

I felt so weak now and every rasping breath I took was agonisingly painful. Then, mercifully, we stopped. I could just about make out the outline of a group of tents with a man stood before them.

Chapter 21

It had been three days since Liam had seen the old man. He'd had to travel south to stay with relatives while his mother attended a friend's wedding. He'd been bored and restless during the entire weekend and could think of nothing else but the old man's plane crash. Had the Germans captured him? Who was the man outside the tent? How badly had the old man been injured? He'd wanted to find out the answers on Friday night but it had grown dark and he hadn't dared defy his mother and stay out late. The scar certainly made sense now.

The old man was certainly a remarkable character. Liam hadn't ever met anyone quite like it. He was gentle and kind-hearted but with a steely interior too. Behind those blue eyes was a man who must have witnessed terrible things, yet he spoke with such a calm assurance and clarity that you couldn't help become mesmerised by what he was saying and falling under his spell.

It was a dreary Monday afternoon when Liam was able to rush home from school and knock on the old man's door. It wasn't long before they were sat in front of the fire. Liam felt more comfortable in the old man's company now and didn't waste any time in blurting out his questions.

"The forest," he said. "In the forest you said there was a man outside a tent. Who was that? Did he help you? Did you escape and get back to England?

The old man sat forward and his piercing eyes seemed to sparkle a little.

"I don't just give up easily you know," he said. "I'm still a resilient old git now, let alone when I was young and fit. Anyway, escaping was only the beginning of the battle."

With that, he took a sip of his ginger beer and began to talk.

It was nicknamed 'the forest of hidden men'. Today the forest is a tangled mass of trees and underbrush, just a lonely stretch of wilderness, not far from the border that divided Belgium and Germany but in the 1940s it was home to one of the most successful schemes to hide allied airmen who had been shot down. It was incredible really. We were able to hide from the Germans in the most unlikely of places – right under their noses.

The man standing in front of the tent was called Jean de Villiers, a soldier who had been wounded during the German invasion of his country. Jean had joined the Belgian Resistance soon after, becoming one of its most daring figures. This was an underground organisation that would do everything possible to disrupt the enemy's plans and help the allies to victory. It was incredibly dangerous. Anyone suspected of being part of the Resistance would be taken away immediately to face a firing squad.

Yes – Jean was an amazing man. Totally fearless. He was slightly eccentric I suppose, with long, flowing black hair and spectacles that were often balanced on the end of his nose but he commanded respect through his actions. He was the organiser of a famous escape line that ran through Belgium and France and across the Pyrenees, before reaching the safety of Spain. Deep within the forest, he had constructed a camp designed to conceal downed airmen like me, before eventually helping them return to the UK.

We'd been incredibly fortunate to reach the camp in the first place. A week or so later, once I'd recovered a little, Stan filled me in on the whole story. Although I had been badly wounded in the crash, he had been relatively unscathed apart from a few nasty cuts and bruises to go with a grazed arm that a bullet had nicked. It gave us a chance. We were on the move almost immediately, with me resting over Stan's shoulders. He had bandaged my head as best as he could but the bleeding hadn't stopped. We'd crossed two fields before we were spotted by a local farmer. He looked up and down the small road where the farmhouse lay before ushering us around the back of the building and making sure we were out of sight.

It was far too dangerous to stay so close to the site of the plane crash and despite my injuries, we would have to move quickly or risk being captured. We were in luck. Just a short distance away, lived a key member of the Belgian Resistance. He and his son had arrived with us in a matter of minutes, leading us into the woods and eventually reaching the campsite.

I've never felt closer to death than I did that night. I was brought inside one of the tents and had my injuries treated by a nurse who had been allocated to the camp. Apparently, I drifted in and out of consciousness and many of the men, including Stan, didn't think I'd make it through until morning. Like I told you though Liam, I don't give in easily and despite losing a lot of blood, I made it through to the next morning alright. I made the one after that too. Jean even arranged for a Resistance-friendly doctor to come out to the forest and patch me up properly and I began to recover my strength over the next three weeks.

The camp really was a bizarre but strangely wonderful place. Somehow, eight large tents had been squeezed in amongst the dense trees, managing to host about seventy-five men altogether. Some ingenious fellow, who owned a hotel back home, had actually fashioned tables and benches made from trees. He used to joke about making sure his guests had a comfortable five-star experience and I have to admit that life in the camp was far from unbearable. We even had two designated cooks to prepare meals. There were only two rules really. Never make a run for it on your own and never raise your voice. After all, we were often within earshot of German troops.

Stan and I stayed in the camp for three months altogether. It would have been less than that if I hadn't been seriously injured. I felt much better but I still suffered from blinding headaches and, even more alarmingly, from blackouts. They would occur once or twice a week and never lasted for longer than a couple of minutes but it still bothered me considerably. It was a horrible feeling to just lose consciousness without warning. I worried that I may have some sort of permanent brain injury.

I couldn't speak highly enough of the bravery of the

Belgian resistance. At the risk of their own lives, they helped us out as much as possible. They brought food and blankets to the camp whenever possible and even the odd bottle of wine to keep our spirits up. Obviously, we would limit ourselves to a small glass from time to time as it wouldn't be wise to become too raucous and alert any Germans patrols to our position. To relieve our boredom as much as anything else, we organised raiding parties that would sneak out and steal provisions from the local shops. Of course, our friends in the resistance would reimburse the shop owners via anonymous donations.

Chapter 22

Finally, the time came for Stan and I to leave. I must admit that I felt a slight sting of apprehension as it was obviously very dangerous to make the long journey through occupied France and the over the Pyrenees. To be honest with you Liam, I was a little afraid I wouldn't have the strength to make it. Jean tried his best to prepare us for our trip, arranging a tutor to arrive at the camp and give us French lessons, giving us clothes so we could pass as Belgian peasants and forging us the appropriate identification papers. It was now or never.

To begin with, Stan and I were moved to a nearby town called Neerpelt where we actually stayed in a hidden storage room of the local shoe repairer. After a two day-stay here, we were taken to the nearby railway station, meeting a dark haired woman named Annie, who would be our guide to the city of Antwerp. She would buy the train tickets herself, before brushing past us and secretly placing them in our hands. We would then board the same train as her but separately to avoid suspicion.

On arrival at Antwerp we stayed one night at the home of a local cafe owner before moving on with a new guide to the capital city Brussels.

We were met in Brussels by yet another resistance contact and spent the night in her flat. It was part of the escape strategy to continuously move from place to place and to change guides. Before long, we were staying with an elderly lady and her two adult daughters. I'll be forever in the debt of those brave people who helped us. They knew the risks involved and I know that a significant number of them would later lose their lives after being arrested and brutally interrogated by the German Gestapo.

One thing I do remember about staying with the lady in Brussels is managing to take my first bath since the crash. The water wasn't particularly warm but I wasn't too bothered. The journey through Belgium had gone without a hitch and, after a brief stay in a village near the border, we crossed over into occupied France. Of course, we were pleased but I had a horrible feeling that perhaps things were going too smoothly. I was also still suffering from violent headaches.

Our next stop was Paris and for some reason I felt incredibly tense. I hadn't slept well at all for the last three days and I'd convinced myself that we wouldn't make it. I suppose it was the same feeling I explained earlier about aircrew approaching their thirty missions. As you get closer to your goal, the more agitated you get. It feels like you've got more to lose. I think Stan felt the same.

The station at Paris was huge and to my discomfort was also packed with German troops. Stan and I tried to mask our nerves as we moved passed two Nazi officers but they didn't seem too suspicious of us and we were able to board a carriage on the Metro without any real bother. I remember allowing myself to relax for a few minutes.

As we changed trains on the Metro, I must have felt more confident in evading capture as I found myself striding down the platform. In fact, one of our guides had to admonish me for walking like an Englishman and not taking small steps like a Frenchman. A sense of vulnerability returned to me and I made sure I kept my focus.

Stan and I had a guide each and the four of us boarded the train in different carriages. Stan was two carriages ahead of me and we waited somewhat anxiously for departure. For some reason the train wasn't leaving the station. My head was pounding and I could feel another murderous headache coming on. Sitting in my seat with a full view of the corridor, I told myself to stay calm and it would pass. Of all places, I couldn't afford a blackout here.

Suddenly, the moment I had been dreading arrived. There was shouting coming from the platform, accompanied by the sound of heavy boots running. Ten to twelve soldiers were approaching the front of the train and it wasn't long before they were in the corridor. There must have been ten carriages and I was in the ninth. Stan was up ahead in the seventh. I felt sick to the pit of my stomach.

Onwards the soldiers came, checking people's identification papers. Through the first three carriages and swiftly onto the fourth they came. I was certain that the Germans would be able to hear my heart as it was thumping so hard and my head felt like someone was drilling into the centre of my brain. I tried to stay calm and play out in my mind what I would say when asked for my papers. My French accent would need to be convincing.

The first of the soldiers had now reached Stan's carriage. I sat there aghast. There was nothing I could do but wait. To my horror, when the soldier approached him, he spoke in French. Well, Stan obviously didn't understand what he had said so he just sat there tight lipped and handed his false identification over, pretending to be baffled by the German accent. Obviously irritated, the soldier repeated what he had said with a touch more aggression. Stan, just sat there, stone faced. Well I think the guard realised that he wasn't going to get anywhere, gave Stan a withering look while handing back his papers, and moved on.

The first two guards continued until they reached the carriage before mine and I tried desperately to compose myself. I wasn't sure whether to imitate Stan's tactics of feigning confusion or risk my French accent replying to their request for papers. My head pulsed with pain and my eyes felt like they were burning. The tension was unbearable.

Well just as the first German was so close that I could almost smell his breath, there were shouts from the front end of the train. The soldiers nearest to me spun around immediately and ran towards the commotion. It wasn't long before they had dragged some poor fellow off the train and marched him down the platform in unceremonious fashion. Perhaps they'd had a tip off about a resistance guide or another allied airman like me. I'd never find out the answer but at that very moment I have to admit that I was just grateful that I hadn't been discovered. It seems selfish now I suppose but that's how I honestly felt.

A few days later, Stan and I took the train to Dax near the Pyrenees. We were met behind the station by a moustached man who gave us a bicycle each. His name was Florentino and he was an absolute giant with a weather beaten face and powerful, muscular arms. He looked tougher than anyone I'd ever met. Shortly after, we began an exhausting hour ride into the foothills of the mountains that bordered Spain. Although it was tough work, the scenery was stunning and there is a sense of freedom to riding a bike that I certainly appreciated. There were a few nervous moments when we passed by German patrols though and I can't begin to tell you the fear Stan and I had of being captured. We would either be shot or at best, interrogated and thrown in prison. I'd heard some horrible stories of the Gestapo thumbscrew.

Well anyway, by the time the light began to fade, the track we followed became so narrow that you could only ride in single file. There was also a worrying lack of railings to guard sheer drops over the side of the mountains. We were so high up that the sides of the path were lined with snow. It was strangely beautiful and it almost felt like we were on top of the entire world. Both Stan and I were exhausted but neither of us would be the first to stop. Have you ever watched the Tour de France on the Telly Liam? It's the world's greatest bike race. Well, they race through the Pyrenees every year but I'm sure they never go as high as we did.

We finally arrived at a small bungalow type building in the countryside where we would rest for the night. We were both given warm clothing, footwear and a pistol. The following day we would begin an arduous journey into the mountains on foot. I remember staring at the Pyrenees away to the south. They looked impossibly high. Freedom was on the other side. So near, yet so far away.

It was getting late again but Liam couldn't bring himself

to leave now. He'd probably get a rollicking from his mother but he was prepared to risk it to hear more of the story.

"It's getting dark Liam," the old man said, "you'd better get off home before you get in any bother."

Liam shook his head.

"I'm alright for another half hour," he said. "Tell me what happened next. Did Stan come home too? Did you two win any trophies together? I'll bet you won the FA cup didn't you."

The old man hesitated for a moment before smiling gently. "Tomorrow," he said, "I'm taking Sam for a walk out at Thompson Park. Why don't you join us?

Liam got up from his chair and headed towards the door.

"Yes please," he said, "that would be great Jimmy."

Chapter 23

The old man had been as good as his word. He met Liam at the park just after four o'clock. There was a path that surrounded the football pitches, leading all the way past the skateboard ramps and passing by the entrance to St. Michael's church on the opposite side of the playing fields. As Sam chased his old, chewed up tennis ball enthusiastically, the old man's thoughts drifted back to the Pyrenees. He took a deep intake of breath before speaking.

Well, after a good night's sleep at the safe house, the following morning we followed a trail of woodland paths into the mountains. We climbed higher and higher, only stopping for a little food and a drop of Florentino's cognac that he carried on his hip in a small flask. The terrain was unforgiving, with steep, narrow tracks and every step was a struggle. I could see the strain on Stan's face as he gasped for breath in the thinning air. We walked for an exhausting seventeen hours that day although Florentino didn't seem the slightest bit tired. He seemed to know every inch of the mountains and was as much as home on them as the sheep. He was also quite adept in the art of psychology as whenever Stan and I began to wilt, he would casually point out how well the other was doing. Of course, as both of us were fiercely competitive, this always brought about a burst of energy buried somewhere deep within our bodies.

Throughout our journey, we had to be as quiet as possible as Florentino had warned us of increased German security in the region. In the past, the complexity of the terrain had left them unwilling to maintain strict surveillance of the mountains but recent orders from Hitler had forced them to crack down on allied escape lines. Worryingly, arrests had multiplied significantly and guides such as Florentino had either been executed immediately or sent to the dreaded concentration camps.

So, on our second day of walking, we were greeted by a road that was slippery from the previous night's rain and led upwards into a cloudy fog. It took some time for the sun to break through but when it finally did, it allowed us to take in a spectacular view of row upon row of snow capped peaks and grassy valleys. It would have been nice to stop for a while and take in the beauty of our surroundings but despite Stan's complaints about his blistered feet, Florentino insisted that there was no time to rest.

Onwards we climbed towards the top of a huge mountain peak that must have reached at least five thousand feet. The ground was now covered in crispy sheets of snow. Sometimes we fought our way through drifts that were waist deep and both Stan and I were desperately cold. I think that only the promise of a nip of Florentino's cognac kept us going. On the brink of collapse, unable to feel our frozen toes, we reached a small farmhouse and almost fell through the door in exhaustion.

I was completely worn out and must have gone out like a light the minute I lay on my bunk.

Well, a good night's sleep must have done wonders for my aching body, as by the morning, I was completely reinvigorated. Perhaps it was the thought of being so close to freedom – I'm not sure really. After crossing one more peak, we would reach the Spanish border. Stan was full of himself too and talked excitedly of our return to England.

"We're almost there Jim," he said, "This is it. Just one more climb and we've made it. Just one more climb Jim."

I suppose I didn't want to celebrate too soon so I didn't get too carried away but I have to admit that in my heart, I felt we were almost there. We'd come so far and I hoped that one more mountain wouldn't get in our way.

So, with a spring in our step, we set out through the pine trees, following a rocky path towards the mountain peak. We had been walking for no more than twenty minutes when suddenly, without warning, a single gunshot rang out from the valley to our right and Florentino dropped to the floor. There was a gaping wound in his neck and his eyes were blank and lifeless. A sniper's bullet had killed him instantly. In a state of shock and fear, I wheeled round and saw that we had been ambushed by a German patrol. There must have been fifteen or sixteen of them, approximately a hundred metres or so away, the bullets from their automatic weapons soon whistling through the air and pinging against the rocks by our feet.

Breathlessly, we ran for the cover of a thick patch of undergrowth, with the Germans gradually moving up the slope towards us. Taking cover behind a large boulder, Stan and I returned fire, dropping the first of the soldiers to the ground. However, the respite was only brief and another huge volley of gunfire ensured that we were pinned down and trapped. When I finally managed to steal a glance at Stan, I saw his hands were shaking and his eyes were wide with terror.

Leaning back against the boulder, Stan laid down a quick

burst of covering fire.

"When I shoot, you run," he said through gritted teeth. "They won't catch us on the mountains. We can make it if you go now. I'll follow you as soon as I can."

There wasn't any time to argue. Sending shards of rock spiralling high into the air, a grenade exploded no-more than twenty feet in front of us. We would have to move before we were blown to bits.

"NOW!" yelled Stan but I couldn't react at first. I tried but my legs were numb and my head ached with a violent stabbing pain that was worse than anything I'd experienced since the first days after the crash. I have to admit I was afraid too. I'm not ashamed to say it. There's nothing that can prepare you for a moment like that and it took every last ounce of my strength to leap out onto the path and sprint, as fast as my aching lungs would allow me, towards the peak that towered in the distance.

With adrenaline surging through my veins, I pumped my legs powerfully while the bullets fizzed past my head. Risking a glance over my shoulder, I saw Stan racing after me. He seemed to stumble and fall for a moment but managed to drag himself to his feet, running over the brow of a small hill to join me at the bottom of a grassy slope.

For a few brief moments, there was an eirie silence before it was rudely interrupted by the menacing sound of a bullet ricocheting off the rockface behind me after brushing past my right ear. Frantically, we climbed higher up the path and into a cloudy mountain mist. This was truly a godsend and made us less visible to our pursuers. It was vital that we got far enough ahead so that we were out of range of the sniper.

I was surprised to see that Stan seemed to be tiring fast,

wincing with every step he took. On the pitch, he would normally be able to run all day long. Then I noticed the blood. There was a small stain around an entry wound on his back, almost unnoticeable at first. He caught me staring but before I could say anything, he found a burst of energy from somewhere and lumbered on ahead.

We must have climbed for five hundred metres or so before I caught up with him at the base of a rocky ledge. When I did, I found him doubled over, his breathing laboured. The bloodstain was spreading now and I couldn't take my eyes off it. I could see that the bullet had struck him just below the armpit and he was clearly suffering with the pain.

"Stan, you need to rest. Let's stop for a while," I said.

"I think – I think," he wheezed, "I think my lung... I can't – I can't breathe Jim."

Every word he uttered seemed to need maximum effort.

"Stan, I'm not going to leave you," I said. "Let's rest here. They won't find us."

"No – they will. We've got to keep moving," he rasped, and with a loud groan of pain and frustration he set off up the mountain again.

We didn't manage to make it further than a hundred yards before he fell to his knees. It was hopeless. He wasn't going to make it.

Summoning strength that I didn't know I had and ignoring my pulsing head, I lifted Stan onto my shoulders.

"No – no," he croaked through dry, cracked lips.

Ignoring his pleas to leave him, I stumbled on a further two hundred yards up the steep incline until the path became so treacherous that I had to hold the cliff with one hand while balancing Stan on my opposite shoulder.

Step by agonising step, rock by rock, we inched forward, my body numb and weakening by the minute. With trembling legs, I glanced upwards towards the peak of the snow capped mountain. It must have been just four hundred tantalising metres away but the icy terrain made it difficult to keep my footing. As I reached for a foothold to my left, the rock crumbled away and we slipped back down the slope onto the ledge below.

Ignoring a stinging pain coming from my back, I was on my feet within seconds and hoisting Stan back onto my shoulders.

"No Jim – No more," he shouted furiously, with what seemed the last breath in his lungs.

"No Jim. I'm not going any further. No more."

I couldn't leave him – I just couldn't.

I looked him right in the eye and saw something from him that I'd never seen before – acceptance of defeat. He was ghostly pale and his shirt was now soaked in blood.

I sat on the ledge beside him, our backs resting against a large boulder, my arm draped around his shoulder. Taking a pair of binoculars from Stan's backpack, I scanned the rocks below. The mist was clearing and I could see the German soldiers below, gradually working their way towards us. Blinking back tears, I listened to Stan's rattling breath.

"Do you know Jim? This must be the most beautiful place in the world." Stan said quietly.

I looked out at the Pyrenean mountain range that stretched as far as the eye could see. The view was enough to take the breath away. The snow capped peaks that seemed to climb all the way into the clouds, the rugged cliffs and the gorgeous green valley below. I could see what he meant. We sat in silence for a minute or two. I wanted to say so much but I wasn't sure where to start.

Finally, Stan broke the silence.

"I want you to leave me Jim. You can make it to the border on your own. I want you to go. I mean it."

"I'm not going to leave you Stan," I said softly. "Never."

"Jimmy," he rasped. You've been the best friend I could ever have wished for. You've never let me down – ever. Please – let me do this last thing for you. Please Jim."

Gunfire began to strike the rocks below. It was some way away still but the soldiers were getting closer. I looked at Stan's face. His eyes were flickering and I could feel him slipping away. My tears were flowing now and I had no way to stop them.

"Jim," Stan whispered. "Please go. I want you to get back to England and tell my parents what happened to me. I want you to tell them I tried Jimmy."

Biting my lip so hard that it bled, I nodded gently.

"Help me up onto the rock up there," he said, "and hand me my gun."

As gently as I could, I helped him up and positioned him so that he was facing the ground below with his gun in his hand.

"Promise me something Jim," he said quietly. "Promise me you'll make the most of your life. The War will end soon. I'm sure of it. You could play for England one day – even make it to the World Cup. You promise me Jimmy – you make sure you give it your best shot. For me Jimmy – You promise me."

With my voice cracking, I began to climb.

"I promise," I said.

My eyes raw and stinging, I climbed up into the snowy peak above, further and further up into the clouds. I could hear shots ringing out below and recognised the sound of Stan's pistol blasting away and the Germans returning fire. The sound of gunfire filled the air for the next few minutes until finally there was silence. An awful silence. I didn't look back – not yet. At last, in total exhaustion, I reached the top. Taking out the binoculars, I looked down at the ledge below. Stan was slumped on his side surrounded by six or seven Germans. Many more bodies were strewn on the rocks further down the slope.

Watching from above, I saw one of the soldiers bend down and check Stan's neck for a pulse before shaking his head. I knew he was gone.

Chapter 24

Liam had been so engrossed in the old man's story that he had barely noticed that they'd walked around the playing fields and through the entrance of St Michael's Church. The old man stopped beside a small gravestone in the courtyard. They stood there without speaking for what seemed like forever. Liam felt his eyes beginning to water as the old man spoke at last.

"Stan's here now Liam," he said, patting the top of the gravestone. "But don't be too sad. He's back in the North-East where he belongs, close to those who love him. After the war had finished, his body was discovered in a small grave in the mountains. In a rare act of humanity in a dreadful war, the German soldiers had buried him and marked his grave with a hastily fashioned cross. We were able to bring him home. I bet he'd be pleased to be buried next to the playing fields here too. He wouldn't want to be missing out on his football.

Liam stood there looking at the gravestone. He had to bite his lip to stop the tears from flowing. The old man seemed to take an eternity before he began to speak again. It seemed like he was still picturing Stan's death in his mind. Finally he broke the uncomfortable silence.

Do you know Liam, It felt very strange when I finally returned home. I'd managed to cross the Spanish border and after a further few weeks of hiding out in stables and farmhouse lofts, I reached the British embassy in Madrid. It wasn't long before I was safely back in England. I couldn't celebrate though. The memory of watching my best friend dying would never leave me. I also think I was just exhausted, both physically and mentally. To tell the truth Liam, I was utterly miserable and my headaches were getting worse too, arriving with such ferocity that I would often be incapable of even getting out of bed.

Meeting up with Stan's parents again broke my heart but I made sure I visited regularly. It was really hard to see the strain they were under. His mother would often struggle to even make it out of bed, without even eating or speaking to anyone. She was absolutely numb with grief and it was horrible to see this bubbly, cheerful woman become a shadow of her former self. It was so difficult to visit their house and see Stan's smiling face looking back at me from photographs hung on the walls or standing on the mantelpiece. However much it upset me though, I made sure I called round every week.

Sometimes, Stan's father stayed at my house until late in the evening. We just sat and talked for hours about football, family and the war. I began to think about the countless families that must be in a similar state. This war had ruined the lives of so many families across the entire world and I began to experience feelings of self loathing. I couldn't help thinking that I should have died with Stan on that mountain. I hated myself for leaving him to his fate.

Eventually, I went to stay with my mother for a while

and she was great. She seemed happier than I could ever remember, completely unrecognisable from the young woman from my childhood. She hadn't touched a drop of alcohol for years now and although it had been five years since I left home, she looked younger now than she did then.

My mother had naturally been extremely worried after hearing news of my disappearance. She had received a telegram from the RAF explaining my status as missing in action. She had become hysterical at first, overcome with anxiety and convinced that I had been killed. For days she couldn't stop crying and barely left the house. It took all of her strength to avoid drinking a bottle of wine in an effort to forget her pain. The next week had been filled with a burning anger and bitterness that she had not suffered for years but slowly she had found some belief inside her that I had survived.

The six months that I was missing were uncomfortably tough for my mother but she never lost hope. As the weeks passed, she was unable to obtain any information about my disappearance from the RAF. There were no further updates after the initial telegram had been sent and there was no doubt that it was a difficult time. Every time she left the house there were sympathetic smiles from neighbours who clearly didn't share her belief that I was alive.

My mother took heart from many other families being in the same boat. Thousands of airmen had been classified as missing and there were reports emerging of many being held in prisoner of war camps in occupied Europe. She continued to be positive and refused to even contemplate the possibility that I hadn't survived, even when the RAF sent my belongings back to her in a trunk.

It had taken years for my mother to rid herself of feelings of deep despair and it must have been desperately difficult not to return to that dark place when I went missing. She found it hard to sleep in the six months I was gone, often feeling restless and suffering from nightmares. There was always a reoccurring image of me falling through the clouds. Strangely she wouldn't see me in a plane but just me on my own, dropping rapidly towards the ground. The nightmares would always end just as I would strike the ground.

Well, when the news of my survival came through from the British embassy, my mother was unable to control her emotions. She'd never stopped believing that I was alive and now I'd be returning home. For the next two weeks, she never tired of telling the entire neighbourhood how tough her boy was.

The time spent recuperating at my mother's house was extremely important to me and helped rebuild our relationship. We ate dinner together every night, went to the pictures to catch a film and just talked for hours on end. I think we spoke more in those three weeks than we'd usually manage in a year. However, I couldn't shake myself out of my lethargy and I was also becoming more concerned about my head. I'd blacked out three times in the last two weeks and my headaches seemed to be becoming more frequent.

Anyway, four weeks after arriving back in the UK, I

eventually returned to the RAF base in Lincoln. I would be given a medical assessment before returning to active service. To be honest with you, my head was all over the place. I suppose you'd think that anyone with any sense would never want to get into a plane again after being shot out of the sky but in a strange way I was actually looking forward to it. I actually thought it might help with the way I'd been feeling and give me something to focus on. I also think that I may have missed the camaraderie that you have when you're part of a flight crew. Perhaps it was the need to fit in somewhere – to know you're needed and relied upon. I hated the thought of just lying about while others were taking the fight to the Germans.

Well, the results of the medical struck me like a sledgehammer. My head injuries were obviously a concern but somehow I thought that I'd soon get over them. How wrong could I have been? The gash on my head may have healed reasonably well but I had suffered a severe concussion. A bad case of concussion is effectively a form of brain injury and the recovery periods can vary greatly. Most people who suffer a concussion will usually be back to normal in about three months but I had suffered an extremely bad case and this had been made worse by the fact that I hadn't had the appropriate medical care in the aftermath.

The symptoms of concussion are very serious and include headaches, weakness, nausea and loss of balance and co-ordination. Naturally, this did not fit well with flying in an aircraft and dropping bombs in enemy territory.

The doctors were also extremely concerned about second impact syndrome. This basically means the possibility of suffering a second concussion before the first injury has healed. A second brain injury is far more dangerous than a first and I clearly remember the medical staff telling me that my symptoms were so serious that any further knock to the head would be catastrophic.

It had been seven months since the crash and if anything the symptoms I had experienced were getting worse. Anyhow, the doctors were very clear. I was to be discharged from the RAF with immediate effect and be grounded for the rest of the war. To my horror, they dropped another bombshell. There was no way I could ever play football again. How could I keep my promise to Stan now?

Chapter 25

I was stunned. I would never kick a ball in anger again. It seems silly really but even with the war raging throughout Europe, I'd always kept that little bit of belief that I'd resume my career. I couldn't let that dream die away. You need that sort of hope to cling onto I suppose – something to aim for. Since I was a young boy, I'd had my goal of playing for England and I'd come closer than anyone could possibly have imagined. When the war had started, that had been snatched away from me in the cruellest manner but I'd always had that little ray of hope to keep me going. Now it had fizzled out and I had nothing! I'd lost my best friend, had no football, no dream and no purpose. I was devastated!

I knew I was one of the lucky ones. Many of my fellow airmen, including Stan and Mick, would never be able to return to their friends and families. Thousands more were missing and I knew that the majority of them would have perished. Although I'm sure a lot of men would have been delighted to be told that the war was over for them, I just couldn't find any peace of mind. Over the next three or four months I began to unravel.

I shut myself away in my house, drawing the curtains and blocking out the outside world, rarely venturing outside unless it was absolutely necessary. If I'm absolutely honest, even going to the local shop was an effort as I didn't want any sort of social interaction with anyone. I just wanted to be alone but the more alone I was the more lost I felt. That seems strange doesn't it but then it's difficult for me to explain my feelings from that time.

Over the next three months, I completely lost my appetite and on some days I barely ate at all. In next to no time, I had lost a stone in weight. As I was pretty skinny to begin with, this left me looking more or less like a bag of skin and bones. I also began avoiding all of the things I used to enjoy as they would generally involve being around other people. I couldn't bear that. I suppose I just felt like such a failure. I guess the only positive thing I could say about that time of my life was that my headaches eased a little. They still arrived regularly but never with the same ferocity as they had before and my blackouts seemed to have stopped altogether. Still, I couldn't really see any light at the end of the tunnel.

It was a call from Sunderland football club that finally gave me the answer to my problems and a purpose in life again. It was my old coach Paul. He'd been contacted by Stan's father who had expressed his concern at my state of mind. He wanted to stop by and pay me a visit. It seems a horrible thing to say but at first I didn't really want to see him at all. In fact, I was dreading his arrival. I think I probably couldn't bear to him to see what I was becoming. Well anyway, he arrived on Saturday morning and managed to persuade me to take a walk around the local playing fields. I hadn't left the house for three weeks. As we passed by the local youth matches that were taking place, we got talking.

"Look Jim," Paul said as we stood near the pond on the far side of the park, "I'm not going to lie to you. You look flaming awful. I mean – you've barely made it halfway round the park and you're out of breath. You've got to have a word with yourself and get back on track."

"It's not that easy Paul," I said softly. "I know I've been lucky. I know that. It's just – I don't know – I can't really explain it. I just feel trapped somehow and I'm not sure how to get out.

We stood for a moment, with a lazy wind brushing gently against our faces. I watched a small boy feeding the ducks bread while clutching hold of his mother's hand. I wandered if he knew that a dreadful war was going on and found myself envying the way he could enjoy the simple things in life. He seemed so full of life and energy -so full of warmth and hope. All the things I wasn't.

"Your headaches," Paul said, dragging his feet in the dirt. "Do you feel any better? I talked to one of the medics at the club and he said there's a good chance that they'll ease in time as long as you look after yourself a bit better."

"Yeah, they're easing a little," I replied. "I'm still not sleeping well though and I don't usually have the energy to get out of bed in the morning let alone go hiking about with you."

We started walking again, heading past the nearest football pitch where two local under twelve teams were battling away against each other. Although at that particular point in time, I had lost interest in anything to do with football, I couldn't help watching. They went about their game with such energy and commitment, thundering into tackles with as much force as their young bodies could manage and playing as if their lives depended on it. I know it seems pathetic but there were tears welling up in my eyes. I tried to hide them from Paul but it was too late.

"I'm angry Paul," I said. "I'm angry that Stan's gone, I'm angry that I can't dream anymore and I'm angry that I've got nothing to aim for. It's been taken away from me and I'm furious. I can't help it. What good am I now? I'm no use to the RAF, no use to Sunderland – no use to anyone really."

I paused for breath, surprised at my outburst. I wasn't really sure what Paul would think of me. In the back of my mind, I thought he would be disgusted with my self pity, bleating on about my injuries when I'd been spared the further horrors that war would bring. Yes – I'd be sat at home with my feet up while others would be dodging bullets and shrapnel.

It seemed to take forever for him to reply and I certainly wasn't expecting the response I got.

"I understand Jim," he said. "I get it. I'd probably feel the same if I was you but you are going to be of use to someone.

"What do mean?" I questioned, a little puzzled.

"Well, seeing as you haven't been much good at getting yourself out of the house recently, I thought I'd give you the kick up the backside you need."

I stood there, like an idiot, with no clue what he was going on about.

"I've gone and got you a job."

"What?!" I said incredulously.

"A job," he said again, "and you're going to need to get back in shape if you're going to set a good example to people too. No more moping about the house and living on scraps."

"What have you gone and done?" I asked.

"I can't tell you. It's classified information," he said. "I'd get in a whole heap of trouble. You just make sure you have a shower and a shave tonight so you make a good first impression tomorrow."

"Tomorrow?" I said, still in a state of confusion.

"Yes, you start tomorrow," he said with a deadly serious expression. "You're my new youth team coach."

Chapter 26

The very next morning, I began work at Roker Park. I hadn't been back since the crash. They'd invited me to a few games but I'd always made my excuses. I guess I just didn't want to be reminded of what I was losing out on.

I should mention at this time, that although the football league and FA cup competitions were still suspended and their team had been decimated by army conscriptions, Sunderland were still able to field some sort of team in regional competitions during war time. The club was still attracting crowds of 15,000 people on match days and this would have been more if there hadn't been restrictions. I could still feel a buzz about the place when I walked through the gates.

Stan's father had arranged it behind my back. He'd begged the club to find something for me and wouldn't back down until he'd persuaded them to take me on as a coach for the under twelve team. Of course, they were deeply concerned about the injuries I had suffered but he'd managed to convince them that I would be fine as long as I wasn't involved in any physical contact with any of the players. The doctors had already explained that strenuous exercise, not that I was capable of it in my state of fitness, would not be a problem for me.

Well, it wasn't long before I'd settled into my new role

and it was the best thing that could have happened to me. It's not particularly easy keeping control of a large group of ten and eleven year olds but it kept me busy, helped me get back in shape and gave me a sense of belonging again. It made me feel alive.

The first thing I had to work on was becoming much more organised. I had never been left in charge of anything before and it took a bit of getting used to. There's much more to being a football coach than showing up with a whistle, a team sheet and a bag of footballs. Being someone that the kids looked forward to seeing every day required well planned sessions and making sure that I created a positive atmosphere from the very beginning. To do this, I focused very hard on making things fun, ensuring that training was based around skill development rather than brainwashing the kids with too much tactical instruction. I also made sure that I promoted respect for all parties involved, including players, coaches, opposition and referees.

It was also vital to get the right balance between encouragement and discipline. Kids at that age need plenty of support to develop properly and you certainly don't want to knock the confidence out of them. After all, don't all eleven year olds think that they're going to be the best player in the world one day? However, you've also got to make sure the kids don't take advantage of you and play up. It's a really difficult balance and one that the best coaches get right. I worked on the basis of making sure the kids knew who was boss early on but then softening my approach and piling on the praise thereafter. Some would say this works well for footballers of any age.

Finally, I took the time to consider how I could develop teamwork amongst the group. While you never want to stifle creativity and individual expression on the pitch, at some point you have to emphasise the fact that working collectively is the key to success. It's not easy at that age either. Imagine that you have a group of ten kids and just one special toy that they're all eyeing up. You know – perhaps one of those fancy computerised ones they have these days. Then you ask them to share it. Well, that's a bit what it's like when I asked those lads to pass the football to each other. It takes a lot of time and a lot of patience too!

So, yes, Stan's father had got it spot on. He'd understood exactly what I'd needed to find myself again. I suppose I fell in love with football once more and was able to share my passion for sport with the youngsters I was coaching. The more my excitement and enthusiasm for the game returned, the more this rubbed off on them. It was a great time and I felt an awful lot better. I was fitter and stronger than I had been in a while and my headaches had almost disappeared altogether.

Chapter 27

While I was slowly getting my life back on track, the war was spreading rapidly. After beginning in Europe, battles were now being fought in Africa and the Pacific. While I had been missing in action, the Americans had entered the war after the Japanese air-force had launched an astonishing surprise attack on the US Navy base at Pearl harbour. Apparently there had been over three hundred warplanes swooping down from the clouds and obliterating warships at will. The world seemed to be holding its breath as it awaited a response.

Well, anyway, I carried on coaching the kids at Sunderland and it continued to provide me with a great deal of enjoyment. I felt comfortable in the role I'd been given and the club, for their part, were delighted with the job I was doing. As my fitness and health improved further, I became more and more active on the training pitch. My co-ordination and balance began to return and I began to look and feel like an athlete again. However, I always took care to avoid heading the ball or putting myself in any sort of situation that could lead to a knock to the head.

One frosty morning, nine months after I had begun my coaching duties, I took a session focusing on finishing. I'd taken probably about a hundred of these sort of drills before but this is the one that I'll always remember. As I said, my health was returning and I could be more active on the pitch than when I had first taken the job. So that morning I joined in the shooting practice with the kids, showing them how to strike the ball with the laces for power, cut across the ball to allow swerve and use the side of the boot for close range shots. I didn't work with a goalkeeper that day but hung a series of different coloured hoops, positioned at different heights, from the crossbar. I'd get one of the boys to feed the ball in from the side and shout a colour. The idea was then to strike the ball through the relevant hoop. It was a variation on the games Stan and I had played in his back yard when we were growing up.

Well I don't think I've ever struck the ball as well as I did that morning. Everything I hit seemed to whistle through the target hoop and nestle in the net. I'm sure the youngsters were quite impressed, although there was a huge cheer on my final shot of the morning when I slipped on the turf and was left on my backside. I laughed too before getting my own back by making the boys run two laps of the field to finish off!

As I walked off the pitch, I ran into Paul who'd been watching from the relative warmth of the changing rooms.

"You haven't lost your touch have you Jim," he said. "The first team could have done with that kind of finishing on Saturday. Perhaps we might have got more than a nil-nil draw with Middlesbrough."

"Thank you Paul," I replied laughing. "You've got to show the kids that you're worth listening to every now and then."

"That's right," he said, "carry on shooting like that and

you might make a decent professional one day."

I chuckled. "So I'll expect a call from the boss on Friday night shall I, telling me I'll need to clean my boots for the league cup game."

Well, anyway, Paul suddenly stopped laughing.

"Did you ever get a second opinion about your head injuries?" he asked.

I was silent for a moment. He'd caught me a little off guard.

"I'm serious Jimmy, you look like a different bloke from the one who I saw when you first came back to the club.

"Well I'm two stone lighter for a start," I laughed.

"That's true, but joking aside, you don't look like someone who isn't fit to play football. Are you still getting those headaches?"

I began to think Paul might be right. The blackouts had stopped altogether and the headaches were now virtually non-existent. My balance and co-ordination, which had been badly affected by the injury to my head, had returned and I no longer suffered from feelings of nausea and physical weakness. I actually felt like my old self again but I couldn't help remembering the warnings I'd been given about playing football again – any second brain injury would be catastrophic.

"Look," Paul continued after a slightly awkward silence, "I'm friendly with a doctor who plays golf at the same club as me. I'm sure he'd be happy to meet with you Jim. What harm can it do to see him? If he says the football is a no go then so be it – at least you'll know once and for all."

I didn't sleep that night. I couldn't stop thinking about what Paul had said at the training ground. It had taken me some time to accept that my football career was finished and I'd nearly lost myself along the way. Now there was the tiniest glimmer of hope being presented to me but in a strange way I couldn't take that final step and go and see Paul's doctor. I'm still not certain why. I think maybe it was the thought of having that glimmer of hope extinguished before I'd had the chance to dream again. In the end, it took me eight long weeks before I made the visit to the local hospital and subjected myself to a number of tests and examinations. I was called back a week later to discuss the results. I remember the conversation clearly.

The doctor was dead straight with me and you've got to remember that this was a long time ago and brain injuries such as mine were an extremely complex subject. As far as I could see no two people from the medical profession ever seemed to agree on how long a recovery should take. To this day, the football association don't seem certain about the procedures that should be in place to help players who suffer a concussion recover safely.

So anyhow, the doctor's report on my physical condition was mixed. He believed that I had recovered significantly from my initial injury and that the damage I had suffered had not been permanent. However, he wouldn't advise making a return as my head injury had been a severe case and the consequences of receiving a second injury could be extremely serious. He didn't go as far as using the word catastrophic like the RAF doctors but he did leave me in no doubt that I would be taking a gamble with my future health if I were to take many more knocks. I suppose he, like the RAF doctors, didn't want to speculate on a condition that the medical profession had yet to fully understand. Different people seemed to respond in completely different ways and brain injuries were a bit of a mystery. I remember the doctor telling me that it wouldn't be advisable to head the ball any longer either although he did make me chuckle when he told me that Paul had informed him that I never could head the ball properly anyway.

As the years have gone by, I've studied reports about head injuries with interest. There have been a few worrying cases of footballers suffering lasting damage. One former England international died way too young from a progressive brain disease that the pathologist explained was due to repeated low level head injuries. This was mainly from heading the heavy leather footballs that were the norm in my day. I think the medical experts believed that having suffered concussions, even minor ones of nowhere near the significance of my own injury, he had not been given a long enough period for the brain to repair itself. Cases like this really bother me and I wonder if I'd have made a different decision back in 1943, if I'd known what I do now. But anyway, back then, I was prepared to risk further damage and it was agreed that I would return to training with the first team squad. I couldn't wait to make up for lost time. I had a promise to keep.

Chapter 28

If I'm honest with you it was hard at first. Although my skill level was back to where it had been before the war, it took a while to get used to the sheer physicality of top level football. It's one thing being able to control a football or fire it into the corner of the net but doing it while opponents are thundering into challenges against you is another thing altogether. I think I was a bit wary of taking a knock to the head and you can't afford to think like that. You can't afford any hesitation at all or an opponent will sense it and take advantage. Play with no fear or not at all.

I trained with the first team for the last two months of the season but I wasn't ready to make that final push just yet. However, it seems strange to say it but I didn't really mind. I was back doing what I loved and felt like I'd been given a second chance. I was only in my early twenties and there was plenty of time to get my career back on track. Besides, the outcome of the war was still uncertain and no-one could really think too far ahead in those days. You just had to live one day at a time and enjoy life as best you could.

Well, the season ended in June but I resolved to use the summer to get myself in the best possible shape for the new season. For the rest of that month, I got on my bike and rode out into the countryside. Cycling is such a terrific way of strengthening your thigh muscles and increasing you lung power. I supplemented this with leg presses and squats and over the next four weeks I could feel my strength increasing. I also worked on my upper body strength, lifting weights and doing countless sit-ups. By the time pre-season had started, I was one step ahead of my team mates and raring to go. I had found an extra yard of pace and it soon became clear that the boss would select me for the opening match at Roker Park.

Preston were scheduled to be our opponents and the local newspapers were full of my comeback. I was even referred to in some pages as a returned war hero. I have to say I didn't feel like one. The real war heroes were men like my friend Stan who'd given their lives in distant lands fighting for our way of life. So, no– I didn't feel like a hero of any sort. I hated the attention and felt more than a little anxious. I'd have settled for showing up unannounced, playing a reasonably good match and easing myself back into first team football.

Despite the restrictions on crowd sizes during war times, the Roker park crowd made more than enough noise to compensate for the empty spaces on the terraces. Trying hard to swallow my nerves, I walked out of the players' tunnel and into a cauldron of noise. In those days, fans used to carry a football rattle and shake it like crazy when anything exciting happened. Well I swear, to you, when I walked out onto the pitch, it seemed like every fan in the stadium was twirling away with something bordering on a relentless fury. I felt my ears were going to burst and when I looked up and saw the sea of red and white scarves, I felt my heart racing. Then I heard it. The crowd were chanting my name – even the Preston fans. I have to admit there was a lump in my throat as we lined up ready to kick off.

Well, I have to say that during the first twenty minutes of the match, I might as well have been sat up in the stands watching. I was virtually anonymous. Every time I made a run into the channels, the ball seemed to go in the other direction and although I huffed and puffed, the Preston defence were always one step ahead of me. I had to fight hard to overcome the negative thoughts drilling into my head. What if I'd made a mistake in coming back? Had I been away from the game too long? Would I ever be the same player I was before the war?

Sometimes Liam, you can be having an absolute nightmare on the ball but if you put the hard graft in you can still contribute to the team. The fans will be far more patient with a player making mistakes if they can see that you're putting a shift in. Your team-mates will be the same too. They won't appreciate players moping about feeling sorry for themselves just because things aren't going well. So that's how I turned it round against Preston. I grafted, chasing down lost causes and never giving an opponent time on the ball. I played that game as if I'd never play another one and gradually I began to get my touch back.

I might not have got onto the score sheet that day but I did enough to convince people that I could play at the top level again. More importantly, I did enough to convince myself. We ended up beating Preston 2-1 in the end but the score didn't matter. I was back doing what I loved.

Chapter 29

Liam sat on the bench looking across at Stan's gravestone. He wanted to tell the old man how sorry he was that he'd lost his friend. He wanted to tell him how brave he was and how much he admired him. He really hoped that he'd kept his promise to Stan. Somehow, though he didn't want to ask and just sat there in silence.

"It's getting late Liam," the old man said, "we'd better get off home before you get in any bother."

Liam shook his head.

"I'll be fine," he said. "Tell me what happened next. Did you make it to the World Cup? Did you keep your promise?"

The old man smiled gently. "Ok then," he said, "Why don't we stop by at my house on the way home. It's getting a bit chilly. How about I make us a nice hot chocolate to get a bit of warmth back into us?"

Liam got up from the bench and they walked the short distance back to their street. It wasn't long before the old man was settled into his favourite chair and continued his story.

Well, towards the end of 1943, with my football career beginning to blossom again, the tide of war was truly changing. There were no more victories for the Germans or the rest of the Axis powers. Allied ships controlled the waters of the Atlantic, allowing America to send troops to

Britain. It was rumoured that a huge invasion force was being assembled to bring the war to a conclusion. It was exciting news and the end of the war didn't seem so far away any more.

So anyway, as I found my feet in top flight football again, my level of performance began to get better and better. By mid October, I was Sunderland's leading scorer with nine goals and I had also weighed in with five assists. There weren't many forwards in the league with a better record than that. Whenever I walked out on the football pitch, I played with an energy and confidence that I hadn't even had before my injury. If anything, I was a more mature player now, with a greater understanding of tactics and teamwork and I began to play with that feeling of invincibility I'd had in the months before the outbreak of war.

Well, it was a cold January morning when the letter arrived. It hit me like a bolt from the blue, landing right there on the mat in front of me as I walked into the hallway. Immediately, I recognised the three lions crest in the top left corner. It seems stupid now but I think I must have stood there like an idiot for about two minutes before opening it.

Eventually, after tearing it open with trembling fingers, I began to read. It makes me laugh how formal things were in those days and I wonder if today's players get quite the same treatment.

Dear Evans

You are required to play for your country on 3rd February 1944 against Wales. The game will take place at Stamford Bridge. Ensure you report to the ground by 5pm.

There were no pre-match training camps or anything like that but just a strict guide on what I was supposed to do and what I wasn't supposed to do. They were even written under those two headings.

What you must do:
Wear jacket, collar and tie with shoes suitably polished.
Be responsible for your own boots which must be in pristine condition.
Laces must be washed thoroughly with no unseemly mud stains.

What you must not do:
Bring friends into the dressing room under any circumstances.
Leave the stadium without reporting any injuries to the England physio.

These were just two of an exhaustingly long list that I won't bore you with. They still make me chuckle. I suppose it would be okay to take an enemy into the dressing room. Friends – no way sir, but enemies – there was nothing in the rules about an enemy being allowed to change with the England squad. I'd travel to the game would be by third class rail. I would even have to buy my own ticket although the FA stated I would be reimbursed. Can you imagine any of today's superstars travelling to Wembley on the train? It was certainly a case of what you can do for your country rather than what your country can do for you. Perhaps a few of today's players might care to remember that.

But anyway, enough of my whinging. Receiving that letter was the proudest day of my entire life. I really didn't have an inkling that I was anywhere near the England squad and it was just a wonderful surprise. It's difficult to put into words how much this meant to me and I wasted no time in telling just about everyone I knew the good news – teammates, family, neighbours and friends. We all got together at my house for a bit of a party. It was a great night but I couldn't help feeling that the one person I had wanted to share the news with most wasn't there. I'm not a religious person but I really hoped that Stan was watching over us all that day and that he'd be proud of me.

The match at Stamford Bridge was scheduled for three weeks time. In the meantime, I continued to play for Sunderland, although I have to admit I was extremely apprehensive about receiving a knock and ruining my chances of starting for England. To my relief, I managed to come through the next two games with nothing worse than a blister on my big toe. It was just three days before the game when the postman delivered a letter from Stan's father. I can read it to you if you like. Bear with me while I get it out of the drawer. Ah – here it is:

Dear Jim,

I've enclosed a letter that Stan wrote before you left for Padgate for your training. He asked me to give it to you upon your call-up for the England squad, if the worst happened and he didn't make it through the war alive. You see, he always had the utmost faith in your ability Jim. He knew you'd get there. Anyway, here it is.

To my dearest friend Jim,

If you have received this letter, then I know that I will not be there to congratulate you in person, but I want you to know how pleased I am for you and I'm sure that your selection is well deserved. I sincerely hope that you can bang in at least two goals and remain a fixture in the England squad for some time.

I wrote you this letter on the eve of our departure to Padgate although of course I'd rather hoped that you never have to open it. I hope that although I am no longer with you, you haven't forgotten your old pal and will raise a glass to me after the match – whatever the score.

I want you to know that our days growing up together were the best of my life. I will always be grateful to you for the friendship you showed me. Take care of yourself Jim.

Stan

Chapter 30

Do you know Liam, I didn't think I could be any more motivated to play for my country but after reading Stan's letter, I found something extra. I took it with me to the match in my kit bag.

I barely slept the night before the game. I was less than twenty four hours from doing something that I'd dreamt of all my life. Four years ago, I'd been within touching distance before events beyond my control had ripped it away. Just twelve months earlier, I didn't think I'd ever pull on my boots again but now here I was – ready to play for my country. It was like being told you were going to win the lottery at exactly eight o'clock the following day. I don't think anyone can fully understand unless they've been in that situation.

Anyway, like I've mentioned before, crowd sizes were restricted during war times but that didn't matter one bit to me. I may have been beside myself with nerves but I also felt a rush of excitement that I couldn't begin to fully explain. Thankfully, the rest of the squad did their best to make me feel at home which I greatly appreciated. Of course, there wasn't much time to bond and make friends as in those days as we only got together three hours before kick-off.

Arthur Knight, the captain, made a point of sitting next to me as we got changed, reassuring me that there was no pressure on me to succeed and that I should relax and enjoy the occasion. Some hope – my heart seemed to be beating at a thousand times a minute. One bit of advice that I did take from him was not to rush out onto the pitch too quickly and miss out on soaking in the atmosphere. As I walked down the Stamford Bridge tunnel, I closed my eyes and took in the deafening cheers of the crowd. This was what I'd dreamed of since I was a boy. During the national anthem, while singing my heart out, I looked up and studied as many faces in the crowd as possible. The population of London had suffered more than most over the last few years and it was great to see the sheer joy and exhilaration on the faces of people of all ages. I was covered in goosebumps. That's how much it meant to me.

I had been selected to play as an inside right. That's probably a bit like what you might see as an attacking wide player. At every opportunity, I had been asked to cut in from the flank and either fire in shots with my stronger left foot or run at pace at the opposition's full back. Well, from the opening moments of the match, everything just seemed to click into place. The game was only just into its fourth minute when I announced my presence on the international scene.

I received the ball to my feet, right out on the touchline. Roared on by the crowd, I drove infield, accelerating past my marker and striking the ball at goal from about thirty yards. It was an absolute scorcher, with dip and swerve to boot. For a second, I thought it was in but it just didn't quite bend enough and whistled past the post. The Welsh keeper hadn't even moved and there was a collective intake of breath from the crowd.

I may have missed the target but this early passage of play really boosted my confidence. The adrenaline was pumping. Buoyed by the energy of the crowd, I felt like I could take on the world. Mid-way through the first half, we took the lead and I played a major part. Arthur Knight had sprayed one of his long, raking passes out to me and I took it on my chest. With one flick of the outside of my right boot, I surged past the Welsh full back and towards the by-line. Lifting my head up, I saw our big centre forward, Nat Jarvis, thundering in at the back post. Instinctively, I cut my foot under the ball, sending it drifting slowly over the two Welsh centre halves and inviting big Nat to attack it with his head. There was only one outcome and the ball was soon bouncing into the corner of the net. Of course, the crowd went bananas with excitement and the whole place seemed to shake. Big Nat jumped on my back to celebrate and knocked the wind right out of me. I don't think he realised how close he came to finishing my England debut prematurely although I think you would have had to saw off both of my legs before you'd have got me off the pitch that night.

The match was full of end to end action to say the least. By half-time it was 3-2 to us but the Welsh were certainly still in the game. Then, after ten minutes of the second half, I was lurking around the edge of the box looking for a lucky break as we attacked. Right on cue, the ball cannoned off a defender's legs and rolled beautifully into my path. I couldn't have positioned the ball better if I'd placed it myself.

There were a number of players positioned between me and the goal but there was a tiny space that was left unguarded in the bottom left corner. I ended up striking the ball with my left instep, sending a low skidding shot whistling along the ground at lightning speed and into the corner of the net.

Players didn't usually go over the top with our celebrations in those days. An arm raised in recognition was about as exciting as it got and there were certainly no robot dances or shirts ripped off. However, I went absolutely crackers. I don't know what came over me. It was just such an incredible moment for me and I'm not even sure I can adequately describe it to you. When you're playing a match, adrenaline is surging through your veins anyway and then if you are lucky enough to hit the back of the net, it gives you such a moment of exultation that you almost feel a burst of electricity igniting your body. Even after the match has finished, it takes hours before you feel normal again.

Anyhow, the rest of the match seemed to fly past at an unbelievable speed. I continued to cause havoc on the right flank and very nearly added a second goal when a curling effort was well blocked by the Welsh goalkeeper. In the end, my England debut ended up with a 5-3 win and the fans were in fine voice by the time the final whistle arrived. Things couldn't have gone much better for me although there wasn't too much time to celebrate as believe it or not I had a train to catch!

Chapter 31

Well, the war continued into the spring of 1944, and every day you weren't quite sure what tomorrow might bring. Although allied forces were pushing the Germans back towards Berlin, it seemed to be taking longer than everyone expected. Finally, on June 5th 1944, came the day of all days. The D-Day landings, as they became known, remain the largest amphibious assault ever staged.

The Germans knew the attack was imminent as they had heard of the invasion force gathering in England. What they didn't know was where the allies would attack. The first wave of the landings began with the paratroopers. These men were unbelievably brave as it was their job to jump out of a plane at night, into the pitch black darkness and the merciless gunfire from below. Can you even begin to imagine the nerve that takes Liam? I'm not sure I could have done that. Anyway, their job was to capture bridges and destroy enemy targets, paving the way for the ground troops to land on the beaches.

After heavy bombing from planes and warships to soften German defences, a fleet of six thousand ships carrying troops, weapons and tanks approached the five designated landing beaches. In total, one hundred and fifty thousand men, from the UK, USA and Canada would take part in some of the most fearsome fighting ever witnessed. People still talk about it today Liam. Those men were bravest of the brave. What they faced that day was almost unthinkable. Try and picture arriving on a small boat with bullets from machine guns zipping through the air. How would you feel as you waded through water soaked with the blood of soldiers that had arrived five minutes earlier and now floated lifelessly in the water around your feet? What would you do when men are being mown down by a stream of bullets right in front of your eyes? Doesn't bear thinking about does it? It must have been hell on Earth that day.

Anyway, although they suffered horrendous losses, by the end of the day, a famous victory had been achieved. It was considered to be the decisive moment of the war in Europe and the Germans were eventually pushed out of France. Of course, it was exciting news for me and everyone else in the country. The Nazis seemed to be on the brink of collapse and even the most cautious of observers thought that they would surrender by the time autumn arrived.

Well, as 1944 passed by and 1945 arrived, it seemed that many people had misjudged how resilient the Germans were. Fierce fighting engulfed Europe although the allies continued to advance towards Germany, resisting one final counter attack by the enemy in the Ardennes forest in Belgium. Finally, late in April, with Berlin about to fall to the Russians, the news came through that Adolf Hitler had committed suicide. Just a week later, it was all over. The war, in Europe at least, was finished.

Of course, after six years of immense suffering and hardship, the British public's celebrations knew no bounds.

Churchill gave the official announcement of the ceasefire as huge crowds gathered outside, many dressed from head to toe in red, white and blue. Total strangers hugged and kissed each other in sheer joy, fireworks crackled into the night sky and gigantic hokey-cokey lines snaked their way up and down streets. It was truly an astonishing time. Even now, VE day is always remembered as the country vows never to forget those who lost their lives. You've probably learnt about it in school Liam. For me though, the celebrations were muted. I spent the day with Stan's family and making sure we didn't lose sight of what the war had cost us.

Chapter 32

In the years that followed the end of the war, so much had happened. I met my wife, Angie in 1946 and we were married the following year. I know you won't want to hear about any mushy romantic stuff but I did fall head over in heels in love with her from the moment we met at a party. It took me three hours and two glasses of whisky before I plucked up the courage to ask her to dance but to my immense relief and surprise, she said yes. Footballers weren't rich in those days so I still don't know what she saw in me.

Meanwhile, I began to reach my peak as a football player. I scored forty six goals for Sunderland across two seasons which was an outstanding return for a player who wasn't an out-and-out centre forward. I became one of the first names on the team sheet when the England squad was selected and managed to live up to the promise of my goal-scoring debut. I managed to score twelve goals in the twenty-five caps I had amassed by the end of 1949 and was lucky enough to play alongside great players such as Stanley Matthews and Tom Finney.

At the end of this year, I became a father for the first time. Angie gave birth to a beautiful, tiny baby girl. We called her Catherine and she was perfect. It was a wonderful time for me and I thoroughly enjoyed my new role although I don't recall getting much sleep during the first six months of her life. Looking after a baby isn't easy you know Liam.

In 1950, came the proudest moment of my football career. The 1950 World Cup was to be played in Brazil. It had been twelve years since the Italians had lifted the trophy in 1938 and now, for the first time in their history, England would be participating after topping the home nations qualifying group. As I had been a regular in the side for at least five years, it was no great surprise to learn I had been selected but it was still a great thrill to know I would be playing in the World Cup. Almost from the first day I kicked a football, Stan and I had dreamed of lifting the trophy for England. In the weeks before the tournament was due to begin, I often found myself thinking of him. It was still painful knowing that I couldn't share this moment with him.

Finally, I was on a plane to Brazil, ready to play for my country in the World Cup. It did take a few glasses of whisky before I could set foot on the aircraft though and my stomach churned for the entire journey. As I'd taken my seat near the front, I couldn't help thinking back to the last time I'd been in a plane, plummeting towards the ground in our stricken bomber. I'm not going to lie to you Liam; it was tough, but nothing was going to stop me keeping my promise to Stan and I desperately hoped I'd do him proud. It wasn't long before I found myself standing in the tunnel of the famous Maracana stadium in Rio, five minutes away from kicking off against Chile in our first match of the 1950 World Cup. Over 50,000 excited fans roared as we walked out onto the pitch in searing heat. As our national anthem boomed out, I refrained from joining in the enthusiastic rendition of God Save the Queen with the rest of my team-mates, preferring to close my eyes and drink in the atmosphere.

Amongst this cauldron of noise my mind drifted back to my childhood. I saw Stan jumping in to stop Billy Graham beating me to a pulp and I remembered the first time we lined up for the school team together. There was a lump in my throat as I remembered sitting in the kitchen at Stan's house shortly before the war started. He'd been full of excitement about the new season and certain that we would break through into the England squad. As the anthem drew to a close, I fought back tears as I thought of Stan taking the controls of our bomber as I sat there helplessly with a torn parachute. Then we were ready for kick off. I stood in the centre circle with the ball at my feet and before the referee could blow the whistle, I raised both of my hands and pointed to the skies.

Chapter 33

It had been a week since Liam had heard the end of the old man's story although he'd popped round to see him a couple of times after school during the week. He'd been affected by the tale more than he cared to admit. At night, struggling to sleep, he'd found himself thinking of Jimmy and Stan. How awful it must have been to go to war. How desperately sad it must have been for Jimmy to lose a friend so close that he might as well have been a brother. He marvelled at the strength of character they had both shown. It must have taken an enormous amount of determination for Jimmy to fight back from suffering such a serious head injury and make it to the England team. And what about Stan? Liam felt a lump in his throat whenever he thought of him and how the war had cruelly robbed him of his dreams. What a loyal friend he'd been. The sort of friend who'd never let you down. The sort of friend who'd give his life for you.

In a strange way, Liam also felt angry. Jimmy and Stan were heroes and yet they seemed to have been forgotten. To him, Jimmy should be living in a big house in the countryside somewhere with fans stopping him for his autograph. He may not have lifted the World Cup (in fact the 1950 tournament had been a bit of a let-down for the England squad) but he had still played for his country and was a war-hero to boot. Now here he was, living in a small house, having sold off all his medals to help pay the bills. It didn't seem right. Not that Jimmy had seemed too bothered. When Liam had broached this subject he had smiled and said how he preferred the peace and quiet.

Now, on a brisk, clear morning, Stan and Jimmy were on Liam's mind once more as he stood in the centre circle of Thompson Park playing fields. With the ball at his feet, ready to kick off a cup match against St Joseph's Primary School, he thought of Jimmy's words over the last three weeks. Today was a new start for him. He made a silent promise to himself that he'd play for the team and not himself from now on. That's what Stan would have done.

From the very first whistle, Liam put his heart and soul into winning the match. This wasn't unusual for him but today he made the effort to encourage every one of his team-mates, resisting the temptation to criticise errors and trying to lead by example. When the opposition took the lead through a dubious penalty, Liam gritted his teeth, bit his tongue and got on with the game. He made last ditch tackles, carried out lung-bursting runs from box to box and played many sensible, unselfish passes to team-mates.

Two minutes before half-time, Liam arrived late into the opposition's penalty area, just as the ball was rolled back by the centre forward. Striking the ball with every ounce of his strength, he watched it sail past the goalkeeper's despairing dive, clipped the crossbar and nestled into the corner of the net. As his team-mates grabbed him in celebration, Liam saw a familiar figure watching from the touchline with his dog. He had a huge smile painted over his face.

Demons of Dunkirk

'This is an unputdownable adventure story woven around the
evacuation at Dunkirk and then the D-Day landings but from
a different angle in that the boy in the story is a conscientious
objector but can the help he brings to Dunkirk lay his demons to
rest? Packed with historical facts but written as fiction this is a
great aid to pupils studying WW2 but also a thrilling read and
a crucial reminder to children today of what their ancestors did
in preventing what would have resulted in an entirely different
country had the UK been invaded by the Nazis."

Lovereading.co.uk

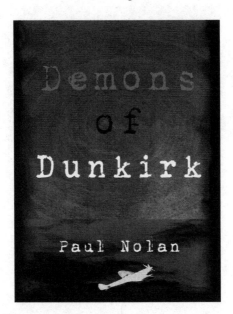

ISBN: 9781906132477   **£7.99**

Attention!

Write your own historical story at

www.creativewritingclub.co.uk

www.creativewritingclub.co.uk